Gudmundur Andrésson is incarcerated in the Blue Tower. With fine wit and rich bawdy he reflects on the calamity his talents, appetites and taste for satirical verse have brought upon him. As a poor but transparently clever boy, Gudmundur is sponsored by a kindly scholar but his desires for high office and a socially advantageous marriage are frustrated by the jealousy and rank-closing of powerful Icelandic families. The birth of a child out of wedlock, counter to the Great Edict – the oppressive morality law imposed by Denmark, the occupying power – and the circulation of a scurrilous thesis seal his fate. Yet ultimately his subversive history is outweighed by his loyalty to his few friends and his intellectual integrity.

The Blue Tower

Published in 1999
by Mare's Nest Publishing
49 Norland Square London W11 4PZ

The Blue Tower
Thórarinn Eldjárn

Copyright © Thórarinn Eldjárn 1996
Translation copyright © Bernard Scudder 1998

Cover image by Jethro, Squid Inc.
Typeset by Agnesi Text Hadleigh Suffolk
Printed and bound by Antony Rowe Ltd Chippenham Wiltshire

ISBN 1 899197 45 1

Brotahöfud was originally published by Forlagid, Reykjavik, Iceland, 1996.
This translation is published by agreement with Vaka Helgafell, Reykjavik, Iceland.

This publication has been facilitated by the generous participation
of the Icelandic Embassy, London.

This book is published with the financial assistance
of the Arts Council of England.

The Blue Tower

Thórarinn Eldjárn

Translated from the Icelandic
by Bernard Scudder

MARE'S NEST

The Great Edict (*Stóridómur*) was a puritan ethical code imposed by the Danish King on his Icelandic subjects in 1564, fourteen years after the Reformation. Prescribing harsh punishments for even the mildest extra-marital misdemeanour, it enabled the Danish King, and equally the Icelandic church and secular officials, to establish tyrannical rule over the farmers who eked out a living from their harsh land. Offenders were punished with brutal and humiliating sentences, the most fearsome of which was being deported for imprisonment in Copenhagen's notorious Blue Tower.

In the seventeenth century the strictures of the Great Edict were ruthlessly enforced, and where the letter of the law did not suffice, witch hunts provided the authorities with whatever grounds they wanted. But ordinary Icelanders clung obstinately to their old ways, their ancient culture – and their instincts. Lore and learning were the only weapons that the poor but literate farmers had against their oppressors, the power of the word which was passed down in manuscripts, stories and poems from one generation to the next.

Gudmundur Andrésson (*c.* 1615–1654) stands out against the age he lived in as both victim and victor: impoverished farmer, poet, scholar, offender against the Great Edict, and accidental escapee from the Blue Tower.

B.S.

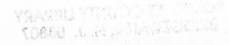

Part One

I am here for the most part alone with my thoughts, because my guards say little to me that I can understand, apart from what concerns my most basic needs. And the same goes for those of my fellow prisoners that I have met; I understand little of what they mean although some of them are garrulous. I had most luck in managing to puzzle out the words of a drunken clergyman who was allowed to go around loose in here for part of the day and wanted to speak Latin when it began to dawn on him that I was a man of learning. But this did not produce particularly constructive discussions, both because that man of God spoke gutturally in the Danish manner when he spoke Latin too, which greatly impaired my understanding of him, and also because he soon fell asleep where he was sitting outside my door and was not long afterwards led away, never to be seen again. He was said to be an adulterer. People come and go here, it seems, apart from me, who only came. I make an exception, too, for the murderer Fredrik, who roams around the tower at his will.

I am also fully on my guard against many of the rabble who drift in here, although doubtless there are black sheep and white sheep in every flock – why should I be the only innocent person to end up inside here? Though I defend my suspiciousness by asking: Could I do anything else after all the tragedies and tribulations that I have suffered at the hands of what are supposed to be God-fearing men? Such slanderers and backbiters are surely found in all walks of life, but perhaps my present brothers and sisters in misfortune could be exonerated by saying that it is a lesser evil to be on one's guard against them than against others who give an honourable impression, like many people who claimed to be good friends of mine, but repeatedly turned out to be the opposite.

A high climb, a short fall. Doesn't that pithily sum up the position I find myself in? I'll be damned if it does. Certainly I never climbed high, though doubtless I aimed a little higher than I ought. Some people thought so, at least. And a short fall? It depends how you look at it: in purely physical terms I have certainly never been higher than now, up here on the fifth floor of the thick and solid Blue Tower, where I have been imprisoned for many weeks. And bear in mind that few of my countrymen ever reach such heights in their lifetimes. *Nota bene*: I mean indoors!

I could go on jokingly glorifying my miserable state to myself by claiming that I enjoy the favour of sitting here in the royal palace as a guest at His Majesty's pleasure, one of the highest-placed people in his chamber. Delusion this may be, but on such a thought I anchored my life when the soldiers led me out of the ship's hold into the dazzling light and I saw for the first time the great city of Copenhagen, as if in sweltering brightness this summer, on that memorable morning of the twenty-second day of July, in this the year of my misfortunes, *anno domini* 1649.

I was seized by a peculiar feeling, so strange that I could not tell in the least whether it was wild rejoicing or the deepest despair. In some way these two feelings co-existed within me, as if these two sensations which have always battled for my mind had finally fallen into each other's arms and established between themselves some kind of accord and equilibrium.

As if pinned between these two emotions, my tormented mind seemed to drain out and a most peculiar calm came over me. I stood there on the deck of the ship between two soldiers who had fetched me from my satanic prison down below. From there, when my eyes adjusted to the brightness, I looked at the incredible bustling crowd of people rippling with chattering, shouts, peals of laughter and wailing across the jetties and beyond, up cobbled streets and squares between houses that towered up into the sky, as far as the eye could see. The

4

soldiers held me firmly by one arm each and made me wait at first while the noblemen, my travelling companions, His Excellency the Governor of Iceland Captain Henrik Bjelke and royal secretary Gabriel Akkeley, disembarked and made their way down the gangplank. I saw those towering figures bid each other a respectful farewell, bowing and scraping with great reverence for each other, then climb into their respective carriages. The doors closed and their ornate coaches rolled away, screeching and bumping, drawn by truly gigantic horses. Not a word of what I had heard about those great creatures was exaggerated.

Since the horses actually turned out to be real, which I would never have believed without seeing it for myself, and since what sounded outlandish was demonstrated to be right and true here, couldn't I just as easily have been brought here as an honorary guest then, rather than the most wretched prisoner of the King? Wasn't it just as likely that their lordships had been sent to Iceland specifically to fetch me? And my thoughts purred away to themselves in this ridiculous delusion: You always wanted to sail abroad, and here you are now. At last, old friend, you have entered all the glory that poverty and humble birth long prevented you from enjoying. Isn't the dream that you always prized above all others coming true, in its own way? How often hadn't I dreamt myself away to this great place once I realized that I was a match in my gift for learning and my sharpness of mind for all the other boys at the Hólar school?

Certainly I was spellbound by all the new and incomparable things I saw. The sun was at its height and it was hotter than I could ever have imagined. Suddenly I began to feel unspeakably good and noticed how my spirits lifted and became cheerful. I was replete, the crew had fed me well at our parting. I felt the crowd was my friend, that I was there like a fish in water, the two soldiers my dearest brothers and companions. We moved onwards in the smell. The smell of food and spices, animals, tar, ale and filth, rot. People. Life.

And when they had brought me – pardon me, when *we* had gone through the palace gate after crossing the bridge that lay over the canal, and finally stopped outside the door of that magnificent tower, my immediate feeling was one of rejoicing. And as if to confirm and underline that joyful emotion, at that very moment a trumpet flourish sounded and drums were beaten in the distance in the palace grounds, to mark some ceremony that was being performed there.

But couldn't it just as easily have been for my sake? asked my erring mind. Those trumpets were tempered in so many registers and the drums were beaten and pounded so firmly and variously that I felt that the instruments which had been blown and beaten so mightily at the Althing Assembly at Thingvellir three weeks before, after the swearing of oaths, and I had considered so magnificent to hear, they merely sounded like whistling and tub-thumping. At this I was finally convinced that I would soon be granted an audience with the worshipful King Fredrik the Third to whom the Icelandic nation had so recently sworn allegiance, and that His Majesty would hardly think twice about rectifying the terrible misunderstanding that had arisen, with a single stroke of his pen, and then compensate me handsomely for the harsh treatment that his underlings had dealt out to me in my innocence. I imagined myself returning home as if in a triumphal chariot, waving a royal pardon in the face of the authorities and everyone I met.

The soldiers knocked on the door and while we were waiting for it to be opened I admired the sight of the palace courtyard, allowing that beautiful music to swell my breast even more. Scouting around, I noticed that the palace was not in fact a single palace but a whole cluster of buildings of various shapes and sizes which formed a circle around the courtyard, with the canal enclosing the whole grand spectacle.

Eventually the doors opened and a stout man beckoned to us to enter, with some words I did not understand. The Danish that those men speak to each other seems completely unlike the language that merchants use with us Icelanders. Others speak nothing but German or various hybrids of it, so at times the language here tends to fuse in one huge melting-pot which is hard for an Icelander to understand.

Inside it was murky and there was a stench in the air. Then when I started hearing distant shouts and cries which seemed to be coming from below us I turned apprehensive and my fit of rejoicing wore off at last. I recalled the accounts given by the God-fearing Jón Ólafsson, who travelled to India, of his stay in the Blue Tower; I once stayed for a few days with Björn from Skardsá at the same time as he was there. Jón described how he had been lowered down by a slender rope into the appalling cavity that they call the Devil's Dike, which by his account was shaped like an egg inside and therefore impossible for any man to escape by natural means. Down there, he said, was a planked floor or large platform, surrounded by deep gutters which drained into the canal. I felt my delusion waning as my thoughts turned there, convinced that I had also been assigned to stay in that lowest and basest of places inside.

We proceeded beyond there, however, along a short corridor and eventually reached a room that seemed to be a kind of watch post for the tower guard, who stood there in person, a scrawny and not unfriendly man, at a lectern.

The stout man turned around and said his farewell, while the tower guard and the soldiers exchanged some papers, discussing them at length and looking over at me every now and again as if to confirm that all their bother involved me. When the soldiers finally thought enough had been done they left too, not wasting much time on saying goodbye to me, their old friend, and left me alone with the tower guard. He squinted at his papers again, looked at me and said in a questioning voice, 'Gunder Andersen?' I, on the other hand, replied as clearly and emphatically as I could, 'Gudmundur Andrésson.' He made several attempts to imitate me, but in vain. Then he shook his head and delivered his final judgement, entering with a clumsy hand in his dog-eared book, as if to confirm who I should be in this place: Gunder Andersen.

I was still wearing the russet travelling-cowl that had covered me in Kaldidalur when the Bishop's evil spies arrested me and took me to the Governor. My cowl had never been an impressive garment anyway, but my subsequent stays in custody at Thingvellir and Bessastadir, along with the hardship I suffered at sea, had by no means made my humble accoutrement any more elegant. But now the guard turned to me, gestured to me to move closer and started searching inside my clothes for something, surely a murderous weapon, clearly feeling a certain repulsion. It was obviously not a task he relished, and he did not search me carefully. Yet he paused when he found the book in my pocket, Apuleius' *Golden Ass*. The guard browsed through the volume, then handed it back to me and said something I took to mean that I could keep it, which apparently was correctly inferred. Eventually he opened the door and called out into the corridor. Thereupon the stout man reappeared, took me by the arm and led me out.

I was almost certain that the moment had come when he would produce his rope, tie a loop around my waist and under my armpits and lower me down into the Dike. He was so heftily built that he could have held the rope with a couple of fingers of one hand with my bones dangling on the other end. But to my astonishment, we headed up rather than down.

Overjoyed at this, I mentally shouted praise for the Lord at being spared from the Devil's Dike, which I later learned need not have been the case at all, since the entrance to that place of torment was on the floor above. However, we were not heading for that floor, but higher up still, until we reached the Church of Darkness, as it was called, where I was put in a windowless, unventilated cell with nothing else to do but flop out and lie on the floor.

For the time being I had been brought to this place, as I later found out, because the guards presumed that some high-ranking official would think it worth interrogating such a dangerous man before allocating him permanent quarters inside or elsewhere. Nothing came of such an inquisition, however, so I was left there only for that first day and the following night, which was none the less quite enough for me.

The first thing that greeted me when the cell was opened was such an abhorrent stench that I almost vomited, brazened though I was by then after my cramped quarters on board the Governor's ship. The reason was obvious. The previous inhabitants of the cell had recently obeyed nature's call in one of the corners; I soon found tangible proof of this while grovelling around for a suitable place to lie down in the darkness from which that church takes its name.

And when I eventually stretched out with the aim of trying to rest, if the tears pouring from my eyes would allow me, I also realized that the soft floor inside there was not earth as I had imagined at first – and in fact been surprised at in a building of such fine masonry – but rather (pardon me the thought) pure human excrement through and through, and it was clearly quite some time since it had last been shovelled out.

It was quite late in the day and I must have dozed off, but woke up again when a panel was pulled back from a hole in the door and I was given a piece of bread and cup of soup which, having no appetite for the time being under these circumstances, I put down on the floor. I would bitterly regret having planned to save those delicacies until later, however, for I soon found out that I had no lack of cellmates who swarmed around when night fell and made a fierce assault on my victuals, which I was not in the mood to defend after that. I mean, of course, the huge rats which the Blue Tower teems with and which start prowling around when night falls and the traffic of the guards slows down.

Not surprisingly, I did not feel sleepy on this first night of mine in the tower, but I called upon the Lord out loud and in silence, in both my native tongue and Latin.

He granted my prayers a hearing, in His infinite mercy, because immediately the next morning I was moved up here to the cell where I have been kept ever since. Although hardly noble quarters, this den is many times less appalling than that awful Church of Darkness. Here, at least, I have been fortunate enough to stay alive since, despite the perils I have often faced to both body and soul.

The arrangement for feeding and starving the prisoners is that someone who has charged someone else and had him incarcerated here while his case is investigated is made responsible for the prisoner's food and keep. So in one sense I have been fortunate, in a manner of speaking, to have been classified as a prisoner of the supreme authorities, because I have thereby been provided with food from the great kitchen on the ground floor of the palace. Admittedly it is no banquet fare, and much of it is strange and alien to an Icelandic palate or has disagreed with my bowels. Bouts of almost incessant diarrhoea have increased my tribulations, ample though they were before, and played their part in withering away the little fat that was on my body anyway. Yet I have been well enough provided for to stay alive so far, whatever may happen now that winter is approaching, for I am starting to fear that their excellencies the authorities have completely forgotten about me.

So I endlessly weave and shape my *Rhymes of the Mind*, like a dog paddling in water. Rack my wits, piece together the fragments.

> No peasant's hovel here befits
> the king's retainer, loyal and true.
> In the royal palace he sits,
> deprived of body's comforts too,
> aspiring here by his own wits –
> Lord Gvendur of the Tower Blue.

know that I would not be here had I not tried to elevate myself above the station in life intended for me. I have seldom been content to yield in silent acquiescence, even if the authorities order it. Presumably I would have fared like Jón Jónsson from Ingveldarstadir, my friend Björn from Skardsá's father, when he sat drinking once with the King's Agent at Bessastadir, which should have been considered a great honour. Jón had left the room to pass water, and when he returned, the Agent spoke these disrespectful words to him: 'Sit down here with me a while yet, my little cock sparrow.' Jón walked straight over to his table and dealt him a mighty blow on the cheek, as he replied, 'If I'm a cock sparrow, I'll ruffle your feathers.' Two northerners who were in the room with Jón rushed for him, and five foreigners were there too. The King's Agent sat in silence for a while, then asked how he could dare strike a royal official in his own room, to which Jón replied undaunted, 'That's to show you that the cock sparrow often soars as high as the eagle.'

At this, the Dane invited him to sit down and drink some more. They were reconciled, but Björn had a suspicion that his father had to hand over something later to soothe his cheek.

Undoubtedly I would have fared better in life had I gladly and gratefully accepted what the Almighty had handed out to me at the start. Which on closer scrutiny was perhaps not so little, I must admit in retrospect, now that I seem deprived of it all. To be sure, my parents were not of high birth nor wealthy, but had reason to feel satisfied compared with what many people have had to suffer in that wretched century. It is fair to say that they were or are – for my

11

mother was still alive when I was taken away – from the more fortunate class of common people who retained some notion of the better life that people had lived centuries before. And as their only son I would, in the course of time, have taken over their little farm unhindered and been able to earn a reasonable living for the rest of my days. But this was not the way that things would turn out, nor did I have any longing to do so. And when I was suddenly driven back there in the end, it was not by my own desire.

I was a very pensive child and continuously racked my brains, in my humble way, about the nature of things. Certainly I was not very old when I seemed to realize that the meaning and sound of words does not always fit the parts of reality that they are supposed to indicate. The fjord where I first saw the light of day *anno domini* 1614 was called Midfjördur, it is true, but could hardly by any stretch of the imagination be considered the most central of fjords in Iceland, to say nothing of the world.

And although the farm was named after a rock and called Bjarg, it became increasingly clear to me when I began to grow up that there was no solid foundation to build upon there for anyone who wanted to rise above wretchedness and the handicap of low birth and poverty, in that harsh land of ignoble men who, generation after generation, had never been half a match for their fathers. At least, I thought so then. I often thought that Tussock would have been a more apposite name for the hovel that I felt it had become. And what is more, the only visible sign of its ancient glory for a long time had been Grettir's Tussock in the meadow. Old people said that beneath it was buried the dis-embodied head of Grettir Ásmundarsson the Strong, the greatest hero that Iceland has ever spawned, who was born and bred at Bjarg in Midfjördur as our old sagas tell.

From my earliest recollections I seemed to have entertained the notion that I was in some way special precisely because I came from the same farm as the great hero Grettir. I soon learned that it was considered a remarkable place, since visitors would always remark upon this, dignitaries and beggars alike. It was not uncommon for me to be sent to point out the tussock to visitors and let them examine and inspect it as they pleased. Such visits became all the more frequent as learned men's interest in the ancient sagas was kindled and spread, so that everyone who cared to know realized that our country was once mainly inhabited by heroes and great men. Generally the visitors would stand and stare at the tussock in reverence, but occasional ones remained unimpressed and said it looked like something that dogs cocked their legs up against. I also remember a drunken clergyman from Skagafjördur who quite shamelessly urinated over it and called it the shrine of heathen dogs, which I saw as clear proof that the man of God had neither read nor heard of that great saga. My temper flared and, despite my tender years, I reprimanded the minister in strong language, with allusions to the saga. He reacted furiously by pointing his yellow foaming spray at me, but missed. For a long time my God-fearing parents claimed this as the first proof of the tendency that would later emerge in me, namely insolence towards people who were considered my betters and my superiors.

Others who saw the tussock said that no one of Grettir's stature could possibly be buried there. This was one of the matters I felt I had to submit to the judgement of Sveinn Jónsson, an old man who was staying on the farm with us and was my first and greatest fountain of wisdom and stories. He had been to school, been ordained long ago and granted a benefice somewhere in the East Fjords, as far as people knew, then lost his holy office through fornication, some people claimed, but others said he had been punished for unbecoming dabbling in the magic arts.

As I later discovered, it was a mixture of both, in a particularly unfortunate manner. While he was a young clergyman, Sveinn had fallen uncontrollably in love with the girl who was deemed the best match in that part of the east, a worthy farmer's daughter. But being an exceptionally bashful man, he did not dare either to speak to her or to look at her, to say nothing of seeking her hand from her parents; was in fact convinced that it was futile to talk of such things. But since his love for the girl grew out of his control, he resorted to trying to turn her affections towards him by magic and hid carved runes under the head of her bed, which delivered their full effect with incredible speed when the girl visited him immediately, panting with passion, and they were consumed at once by a burning love for each other, outside all matrimonial vows. Sveinn believed that this was thanks to his magic, but in fact the girl had noticed him when he was hiding his tokens in her bed. Realizing his feelings for her, she became ecstatic, for she had also been secretly in love with him and had not dared to reveal it for the same kind of bashfulness that plagued Sveinn, and for absolute certainty that it was unrequited.

Her parents, who previously considered the clergyman a fine match, became disturbed at the way their love for each other grew so public and fast and frequent, and they turned against him completely when they heard word of the runes he had carved. In vain the girl pleaded that the runes had played no part in turning her affections towards him; they did not believe her and he could not even be certain himself. At least, the parents always said that he did it anyway.

So it turned out that Sveinn was guilty at once of black magic and fornication, though without producing a child outside wedlock, and he could certainly think himself lucky for not losing more than his benefice. He was unfrocked, while the girl pined away and died.

I did not concern myself with such rumours in my childhood and old Sveinn himself never said a word about what happened, but ever since then he had been working as a journeyman farmhand all over Iceland. He always had a great love for ancient lore and owned a fine trunk full of books that he had never got rid of despite all his wanderings. Inside it, among other things, was an old manuscript copy of *The Saga of Grettir the Strong* and other good works, from which I learned to read; I turned out to be a quick learner and earned both praise and encouragement for it from my parents, neither of whom was literate. My mother in particular made a point that I should try to study, and would often recall how one of her great-great-great-grandfathers had been a clergyman. My father, on the other hand, had a much lower opinion of the written word, and said that many a man had read himself out of his wits. He thought it more important for me to be as useful as possible on the farm, especially since his health was

14

poor and not improving either. Or was his ill health mere endless complaining? Each of them was very fond of me, in their respective ways, since I was their only surviving child.

In my sufferings here I can imagine us now, me and old Sveinn, early one spring time stamping dung into the frozen ground not far from Grettir's Tussock. I see it all in my mind's eye here in my tower prison, but from a distance as though through the eyes of a spectator watching the old man and me taking what seemed to be a peculiarly aimless stroll.

Then I asked, 'Since Grettir's Tussock is here in the meadow, why hasn't anyone dug it up to find out for certain whether the head's really there or not?'

Sveinn replied at once, stopping on the spot, that no one should disturb the rest of the dead. And what purpose would such dabbling serve? Isn't it always better to think you know of the head there, ignoring the uncertainty, rather than to be convinced that it isn't there? And then, if that head came to light as it doubtless would if anyone dug there, how would anyone be better off for it? Just tell me that. What could Godless grave-robbers do with a head like that? Make it tell them something?

I fell silent at once and determined never to confide in the old man about the firm resolution now taking root within me – to break open the tussock one bright spring evening while I was alone watching over the flock of sheep. Perhaps not this spring or the next one, but maybe the one after that, who could tell? I wanted to feel the skull, run my dirty fingers over it. I felt that the head would establish so much. I didn't plan to ask it anything in particular, but felt certain I would be given answers to all I wanted to know if I could sit with that head in my hands and stare into the sockets of its eyes. But for as long as that was impossible I made do by grilling old Sveinn with questions about everything in *Grettir's Saga* that I could not understand.

I mainly asked about the fire Grettir was said to have started in Norway, with which his whole misfortune began. When Grettir entered the house of Thórir's sons and their men and accidentally caused the fire in which they were burned to death inside. He definitely did not do it on purpose. Why was such fierce revenge taken on him, then, for something he obviously had not planned to do, and was therefore not a misdeed?

I sometimes had the feeling that the old fellow had been on speaking terms with all the heroes of ancient times. He knew all their sagas so well. But to questions such as the ones I continually burned to know about, he could only answer with his incessant proverbs: Fate can never be opposed. Fate and Fortune never go hand in hand.

I went on hammering the point: when Grettir was sentenced to outlawry, why didn't he just go abroad to seek the fame he was born to achieve, rather than roam the mountains and deserts on the border of the habitable world, pursued like a dog, hemmed in like a fox in its den? It was then that he genuinely became a thief and criminal. Why couldn't he rise to the challenge and leave Iceland as quickly as he could? Don't you reckon that Grettir, hero that he was, couldn't quite easily have found his way to Constantinople, where all valiant men touched down, just like his brother Thorsteinn did? Who could tell then whether he wouldn't have won the Lady Spes, who later married his brother, and would have brought her back after those twenty filthy years to settle down as a free man here at Bjarg?

'Could have, should have,' the old man muttered. 'The saga's extremely clear on that point: it never was, it never happened. My lad, you talk as though the saga-writer arranged it all for himself and could have changed other people's fates and fortunes by himself.'

Then he pottered off bow-legged to the next heap of dung and began stamping it into the ground, twice as vigorously as before.

I followed him, but before I knew it I had started kicking the dung all around me with a strange aggression, as if seized by a wild frenzy. I stamped on the pellets of dung as if I were battling with my arch enemy.

And to think that my mother was called Ásdís, just like Grettir's. Couldn't it easily be the same family? Probably not direct descendants, because the saga says that Skeggi, Grettir's son by the widow Steinvör from Sandhaugar, died at the age of seventeen. But who could tell how precocious a lad he might have been? And Grettir, who called it a trifling job for weaklings to look after geese, what would he have thought about our task of spreading dung? And why should I have to put up with this instead of rebelling the way Grettir did when he grew bored and flayed the hide off a mare's back, in the hope that she would feel the cold and go back home? Or when he ran a wool comb across his father's back because he thought it belittling to have to sit around scratching the old duffer like some beggarwoman?

But that just wasn't the way things were any more, I could tell that. It was a different age now. I couldn't possibly imagine how something like that could happen, could scarcely envisage what punishment would await me, and quite rightly too, were I to deal out such Godless and harsh treatment to an innocent creature.

Nor had I ever noticed that my father liked having his back scratched. And it would definitely have finished him off for good if I had taken a deadly weapon like a wool comb to him as he sat hunched over on one of those cold mornings, bronchitic and coughing. Moaning and groaning.

My cell here in the Blue Tower measures two and a half of my strides wide, and I can cross its length in four strides. But what most distinguishes this place of abode from the tribulations of the Church of Darkness where I spent my first night in the tower, is that daylight pours in through the window which is situated high up in one of the longer walls. The window alcove measures more than two ells long, or rather deep, since the walls are so thick in this mighty tower. It can be said that it rather depends on the season of the year whether the window represents a blessing or an ordeal. The blessing predominates, though: the daylight, together with less fetid air, outweighs the ordeals posed by the cold now that winter is approaching; there is neither glass nor a screen across the window, so it is always open.

Not very long after I had arrived here, the guards reappeared and brought me a battered old bed along with a poor mattress and a blanket of sorts. I can stand the bed up on its edge and use it as a ladder to reach the window, where I feel happier than anywhere else, sitting up there at length and often reading for my pleasure the only book I have to hand, Apuleius' *Golden Ass*, which I was carrying with me when I was manhandled by those rogues in Kaldidalur. I would even attempt to translate that tragicomic story into the Icelandic tongue if I had pen, ink and paper.

It is no less a pleasure and diversion for me to have some view from my window, in fact mainly of the roof below where some of the palace buildings adjoin the tower. Thick iron bars have been put across the window, but the gap between them is adequate for me to stick my head through easily, and since I am not heftily built I have no trouble in slipping my body through either. Because the bars are not placed on the very edge, but are set some way into the wall with a steep sloping surface beyond them, nothing but a fall to the death would greet any man who saw this as offering easy means of escape from the prison. But by lying down on the inside of the window alcove and thrusting my head and trunk out between the bars, I can gain a better view beyond the wall, and prevent myself from falling out by gripping those great iron bars with all my might. I can in fact see over a fair part of the palace grounds then, but it is disapproved of if I reveal myself in this way in broad daylight and I have not attempted to do so after being sharply rebuked once and threatened with confinement in the Devil's Dike if I were discovered hanging out of the window again when the King himself or his noble foreign guests happened to pass through the palace grounds. What is not objected to, however, since no one can see me by cover of night, is if I lie on my back and thrust myself out in the same way to examine the stars and the movements of the constellations, which has long been my entertainment in the evenings.

If I thrust myself out like this and keep a tight grip on the thick bars I can look up diagonally at the sky from beneath the outer edge of the window. Though not more than a few seconds at a time, since the strength soon drains from my arms if I perform this act for too long at once. This view of the stars has been like nourishment for my spirit, giving me access to a paramount feat of creation and likewise offering some kind of consolation to know of people back in Iceland who are perhaps looking at that same instant at those same stars.

Then I think of all the people who have treated me best, and wish that no evil will ever befall them. I think of my aged and honourable mother back home at Bjarg and my loyal friend Einar Arnfinnsson, clergyman at Stadur in Hrutafjördur. I think of Björn from Skardsá and my friend Hallgrímur Pétursson, clergyman at Hvalsnes, and his wife Gudrídur.

Not least, I think of Frída and my boy, wherever they may be and whether they are alive or dead, either or both of them.

Sometimes I think, too, of Sigrídur from Stadarbakki and in anguish I see before me all that might have been, had fortune wanted to flatter me by disarming my opponents and thwarting all their efforts.

Yet I still have to put my faith in the Lord. Whatever may be said about the many questions I raised in my discourse against the Great Edict, it ought to be as clear as day to anyone who takes an unprejudiced approach that its main content and foundation are the express opinion put forward in the lawful reply of the Lord's Apostles, in Acts 5, to obey God rather than men. That wherever the laws of God and of man disagree, then the law of God shall prevail, and the law of man yield. This truth has, admittedly, been abused before and since by the Papacy, which called its decretals and pronouncements the law of God, but which is a complete distortion. The Pope is no true God, and his traditions and pronouncements are therefore no laws of God, if God's commandments conflict with them.

I have asked who is wiser than God to know what is most right. Who has rightful vision such as God to see the most suitable order of things? Who has power to impose laws on creatures, like the Creator Himself? I certainly said: It is neither the Bishop of Rome, the Pope, nor any Icelandic prelate and least of all twenty-four uneducated laymen, like the promulgators of the Great Edict, gathered together in *anno domini* 1564 beside the river Öxará in south Iceland. How such people had the power to impose that edict upon the bedroom habits of us Icelanders I have never been able to fathom.

Item, I do not clearly understand or perceive how that edict can be in accordance with God's words or His laws. My aim in writing my discourse was simply to induce the good-hearted reader to speculate with me and consider whether God's law and the law of our land in any respect disagreed, so that the verse that God's law shall be above that of men would need to settle the difference between them. Or whether people who are subjected to such law have the possibility of appealing to God's law in order to protest against the law of man.

And since man is said to be a rational animal, having the power of discourse and inquiry to deduce and prove one thing by another, I felt

I could trust that his sensible head would find it neither base nor improper to contemplate the truth. For truth emerges most clearly when a question is attacked and defended. We test the strength of iron with an iron file. Glass breaks when bent, but gold is shaped. A headwind makes the storm stronger.

In particular, I asked that the authorities should tolerate the truth when it was stated, the reader augment what was understated and everyone contemplate what was questioned. That people should gladly and freely indulge themselves in a little mental gymnastics. Just like the late Jón from Ingveldarstadir, I believed that children always enjoyed hearing how the cock sparrow sported with the eagle on the wing, sitting on its back and saying, 'Here I am!'

have often been reprimanded in the course of my life for an excessive tendency to ponder things that are better left untouched. Many people who have made my acquaintance have claimed that this is the root of various predicaments that have come upon me, the *summa summarum* of which is the great misfortune that I have now wandered into and see no end to. All this may be true, for what was my humble self doing in attacking such a Great Edict, the law imposed upon us Icelanders last century that we might all the more quickly abandon our alleged longing for incest, adultery and fornication. My writings are, of course, the immediate reason that I was transported here, but in many ways they are more a convenient pretext for my envious and ill-intentioned adversaries to take belated revenge for my alleged misdeeds towards them – all of which, if there ever were any, had long ago been paid for by expelling me from my office and prohibiting me from taking either the cloth or a wife. I nurtured bitter feelings about this, and saw common people treated so badly by the law that I was prompted to compose my *Discursus oppositivus*, demonstrating in full that the edict was in no way the work of God, and therefore nothing but unlawfulness.

But those who should have known best of all that I was right, such as many leading clerics and men versed in law, merely shook their heads; they called me mad to ponder such things and foolhardy to attack, alone and unsupported, legislation agreed and signed by the Assembly and the King. But to tell the truth, the Danish part in making that unlawful law is very much exaggerated. Like many awful-tasting things, the mighty potion of the Great Edict is largely home-brewed. Thus I wrote in the love song of my *Sixth Ballad of Perseus*:

> Fate comes from above to here,
> fortune hovers all about,
> curses from a place we fear,
> lawlessness from home sets out.

Some people wanted to interpret my writings as vanity and mere longing to boast of my learning. Such slanderers disregard the fact that my *Discursus*, despite its Latin name, is written largely in pure Icelandic. Had my motive been to display my learning, would I not have written it rather in Latin, if not Greek or even Hebrew?

A ponderer, these same people wanted to call me. A ponderous ponderer was the phrase that Thórdur Jónsson, Archdeacon of Hítardalur, used to describe me to my own face once last winter when we chanced to meet and disputed at length about the Great Edict. Though he called me that, he later confided to me that in his heart he agreed with me in most respects about the evil edict. But said it was dangerous to follow such arguments too far. Anyone who immersed himself too deeply in such treacherous soil could end up six feet under before he knew it.

I never did dig up the tussock back home at Bjarg. Perhaps old Sveinn's strict admonitions were enough for me to abandon the scheme; when we discussed the matter he was continually citing from his ever-flowing store of proverbs: You don't know what you've had until it's gone. Or: A head in a tussock is better than none in the hand, to mention a few. As it happened, I never gave up the idea of digging to find the head, but merely kept on postponing it, incessantly, and I even still believe that I shall do it yet. Perhaps I should resolve right here and now to make that my first job if I ever leave this dungeon alive and return to my native country. This I hereby declare, if it be God's will.

But though I left the tussock undug, I buried myself all the deeper still in *The Saga of Grettir the Strong*, then everything else from antiquity, one work after the next, some of them rotten and mouldy manuscripts that Sveinn kept in his trunk full of books, as I became all the more skilled in reading and understanding. And it all confirmed to me the bitter truth of how everything in Iceland had been so much grander and better in times of old than seemed to be the case in our present age.

My thoughts genuinely began to revolve around whether I would ever have the chance in my life to devote myself to books and scholarship. I dreamt of going to the cathedral school at Hólar, but on first impression I did not seem to stand the slightest chance, for every able hand was needed on my parents' farm, particularly with the state of my father's health. And as I began to grow up, for all my dreams and fantasies, I willingly undertook all the tasks there like everybody else, never sparing myself. From an early age I was vigorous and tough and invariably surprised people with my strength, considering how small I was, like the rest of my family. This was particularly true at the fishing camp, when I joined the fishing boats. Strangers were always joking about what a kitten like me wanted to do at sea, but they found a different story and I had nothing to blush about in front of such arrogant characters when our dealings were over. I was not least noted for how boldly I could answer insults, and I was probably considered malicious by the many victims who were burnt with the lash of my sharp tongue. Likewise I trained myself in composing lampoons about people who tried to provoke me, which did not serve to boost my popularity but gave many an oaf a much needed lesson in the time-honoured art of buttoning one's lip.

Soon I also began to acquire something of a reputation for sorcery, as often happens to those who meddle in books. And more so because old Sveinn had taught me the runes at an early age, admittedly not for magical purposes – once bitten, twice shy – but merely to explain them like any other alphabet. For my part, I did little to shake off this reputation, though I was cautious and never went so far as to suffer for it, and always avoided making tangible proof such as carvings or healing signs and the like. In this way I avoided ending up on the witches' pyre, to be sure, as so many tricksters have done and still do in our superstitious age. But I soon found out that with such a reputation about me I could keep braggarts at bay, and sometimes I needed to. Eventually this rebounded on me, like so much else, when I was smeared with the slander that brought me down.

All kinds of exposure to the elements built me up in many ways, though I still always looked puny. I grew incredibly tough, learned to use tobacco and spirits for the major benefit of my health, and could keep up with anyone at this even at an early age. I also bought large quantities from merchants, *item* foreign fishermen, if I had the chance, and resold them at the customary extortionate price. I established a regular clientele among farmers and clergyman and earned a pretty penny, though I drew sideways glances for it, to which I paid no attention. My clearest feeling of all, however, was that I could never content myself with the fishing-camp life indefinitely.

My chance came when divine providence chose to engineer my personal acquaintance with the greatest man in Iceland then, the nation's finest son, who later became like a patron to me; one of the few people of our day who can be said to have approached the mental accomplishments of Iceland's ancient settlers. This was that grand figure of spirit and scholarship, the Reverend Arngrímur Jónsson the Learned, our neighbour, Archdeacon of Melstadur in Midfjördur, truly Iceland's guiding light and also its champion when ignoble men abroad tried to heap abuse and ridicule on it, like that Dutch slob Dithmar Blefken.

While I was growing up I was hardly aware that the Reverend Arngrímur lived in the district, since the parish church for Bjarg was at Stadarbakki and not at Melstadur. Besides, the Archdeacon always spent long periods away from home, not infrequently at Hólar working on scholarship or other duties such as the three or four years when he was appointed acting Bishop after sickness claimed the life of his relative and foster-father Bishop Gudbrandur Thorláksson. He had been appointed official to the See in 1627 on the death of the Bishop, who had suggested him as his successor. But it turned out that the Reverend Arngrímur, by an unfortunate accident, failed to win the actual title of Bishop, which instead, unfortunately, ended up in the hands of Thorlákur Skúlason. On account of his long absences from Melstadur, Arngrímur had to keep chaplains there, not exactly the most trustworthy of characters.

At this point it was the year 1631, when I was in my seventeenth year. The Reverend Arngrímur was beginning to show his age, at sixty-three with his health steadily deteriorating. He was spending more time at home then than before, though he continued to maintain a chaplain at great expense, in particular in order to be able to devote himself to ancient lore, of which he was fondest of all things. He was no farmer, though he liked to involve himself in running his farm; this meant that he had trouble keeping stewards and farmhands there, for which reason he sometimes had to put up with nosy and subversive characters who more often than not were themselves later forced to leave on account of incompetence. And though the Archdeacon had enjoyed rents since olden times from a good many farms belonging to the See at Hólar, in return for his scholarship on behalf of the Danish Court Historian, he still sorely needed everything that his own farm could produce. He had a large household to maintain, having remarried not many years before, and his new wife was giving birth to one child after the next around this time and some while afterwards.

This was the situation there when Arngrímur's former chaplain for several years, the Reverend Illugi, whom I often helped to procure spirits and tobacco, mentioned to me one winter that I should go to Melstadur to work as a paid farmhand for the summer, and since my father was in fine health at the time this was settled. I went there with considerable expectations, though I could not hope to find anything awaiting me there other than the usual toil. That was there too, but at the same time something else awaited me which I took to be my greatest stroke of luck ever – but was it? I must surely ask this question now that I find myself in such wretched straits here in this evil place, even though it is part of the place of the King himself.

A learned leader of men such as the Reverend Arngrímur could never have been expected to pay the slightest attention to a wretched farmhand and crofter's son, but that is what happened all the same, and the background was as follows. I had taken only a few humble possessions with me from Bjarg to my new place of residence, since it was a short way to go back home if the chance arose, but there was one thing that I made sure not to leave behind, and that was my dear departed friend Sveinn's library, which had been passed on to me after his day, and continued to be my greatest refuge and love in all my free moments and perhaps some stolen ones too. I would either absorb myself in the sagas for yet another time, or pore over the cryptic poems that were in Sveinn's trunk in abundance, or I would read without understanding, or at least look at, texts in Latin that Sveinn had amassed while at school by copying them out from other books. Among them was what I soon realized to be the Latin grammar named after Donatus, which I had heard boys from the school refer to among themselves as the Donat.

Perhaps inspired by vanity, it was precisely such reading matter that I was poring over to while away the time during a break from work, and instead of lying indoors in the sitting room I had chosen to do this outdoors under the hayfield wall in the fine weather. I studied away and had completely forgotten myself until a shadow blocked out the sun and I looked up to see Archdeacon Arngrímur there in person, having gone outside for his constitutional, in a deep reverie that nothing could disturb until he suddenly caught sight of my unworthy form where I lay huddled up beneath the wall with a book in my hand. He overshadowed me and stood still for a while, fat and respectable, with an expression full of character, then ordered me curtly to hand over what I was reading, asking whether I might have been stealing volumes from his private *bibliothèque* which he had set up in the church attic.

Impulsiveness has always been one of my traits, especially with my tendency to flare up when spoken to sharply and not guard my tongue in replying. I flew into an instant rage and, base lad that I was, spat out at the honourable Archdeacon that it wasn't any of his damned business what I chose to occupy myself with by reading in my free time when I felt like it.

The Reverend Arngrímur was widely considered a pompous and

haughty man, and so he was, though I later learned another side to his character, and he clearly would not allow such insolence and arrogance as I had shown him to pass by without reproach. He brandished his stick and struck the book from my hands, but I reacted more wildly still and managed to get my hand to it where it lay on the ground before Arngrímur did, since he was fairly stiff and ponderous with age, and he cracked and creaked, farted and groaned when he tried to bend down for the book. But if angry at first, I was even more furious at being struck. Without a moment's thought I snatched my book up from the ground in a rage, leapt up on to the wall and broke into a spurt along it, I did not know where.

The Reverend Arngrímur followed in pursuit, shouting and calling out, so that people all over the place looked up. Two of his sons from his first marriage happened to be near by, Jón and Gunnar; they had just arrived at Melstadur to accompany their father to the Althing. When they heard their archdeaconly begetter shouting so loudly they obeyed the call of family duty and rushed after me alongside the wall I was running on. Because they were fleeter of foot than the elderly man of God, they managed to grab me before I could jump down from the wall. If I had succeeded in doing that, it was almost certain that I would soon have shaken the brothers off, being so much nimbler and lighter.

And having nabbed me they held me tight until the worshipful Reverend Arngrímur arrived at last, puffing and panting, and snatched the book from me. But he saw at once, of course, that this was no booty spirited away from his own library, but rather old Sveinn's tatty, grimy and ancient copy of Donatus. As soon as Arngrímur realized this his anger gave way to astonishment that a helpless, base farmhand should have such leanings. And when, in this bewilderment, he discovered that his labourer did not own only this scruffy book, but also spent long hours poring over a whole trunk full of them, he wanted to take a look in the trunk immediately, and found there among other things what he described as a rare version of *The Saga of Grettir the Strong* itself. As a result of this incident he offered to give me some elementary teaching if I would stay on and work on the farm at Melstadur that winter.

My parents urged me to accept this offer, not least my mother, who had long ago noticed my love of books. Perhaps she suspected that such an arrangement might, in the course of time, help me in being admitted to the school where she knew my aspirations lay. So it was settled that I would stay on at Melstadur the following winter, and in all I spent three years there.

nce I realized that I would not be leaving this place in the immediate future, I greatly feared at first that I might sink once again into the same abyss of madness and despair where I had sometimes dwelt before in adversity. But when I felt within me another and even worse dungeon, I thought to myself that, as the Danes say, the half of it would be quite enough. I sensed that my life was at stake and that here in this place all my efforts had to be directed towards simply surviving, whatever happened afterwards. With God's help I have managed to hold on tight to that thought, and in this way in particular I have succeeded in staying afloat and staving off the despair that, none the less, I have had ample cause to succumb to.

At first I intended to keep myself amused during those long days by composing poems and ballads and committing them firmly to memory as an intellectual exercise, but little has come of that. I have thoroughly proved on myself the truth of what my friend Hallgrímur Pétursson, clergyman in Hvalsnes, once wrote:

No one can work a word of verse
when his thoughts by cares are harried.
His mind drifts forward and reverse
like a ship on the waves is carried.

Yes, I have experienced that as my mind drifts back and forth in here brooding over all that I have been through. Yet it has been great consolation to me to try to assemble some kind of picture of what happened. Then I address my words either to my own self, the walls

30

here, or a poor old rat that sometimes creeps in to me by cover of night, or then my lost son who would soon be two years old if by some improbable chance he were still alive somewhere in my rough and harsh fatherland.

I have also adopted the device of recalling some of the poetry, ancient and recent, my own and other people's, which I have learned in the course of time. Also passages from the Holy Scriptures and all manner of learned things that I have committed to memory as best I could at school and later.

During my third year at Melstadur, the Reverend Arngrímur first broached the subject of whether it was not right and deserving for me to go to school. The day that he mentioned this first I considered for a long time to be the most joyous day I had ever lived. All my hopes and longings had been directed at this for so long, but despite my alleged impulsiveness I had never dared so much as snatch a glance in that direction, on account of my poverty and lowly background. On the other hand, I was equally aware after my studies during the previous winters under Arngrímur's secure wing that I had at least as much reason to go to the school as many others who wandered in there as snivelling infants, mainly on account of their parentage and not because they had shown any particular predilections in that direction.

Not only had I already acquired a good command of various basics, including both Latin and theology, but I had also become a close helper of Arngrímur's, and almost essential to him for copying out many old things which he wished to study. I felt that I had become in effect his private secretary, alongside my labouring work on the farm. Improbably enough, at least considering our first acquaintance, the closest of friendships developed between the learned and honourable Archdeacon and his wretched labourer who could not have expected any more at first than to swallow the odd crumb that might drop from that renowned man's table of plenty. The Archdeacon did not reveal our friendship to other men of high rank, but always kept me at an appropriate distance when such people were around. I proved so useful to him that he let me ride to the Althing with him the last two summers.

Our bond of friendship grew firmer and much closer when the farmhand's particularly expedite and direct means for providing copious quantities of tobacco and spirits came to light, which I remained exceptionally vigorous and resourceful in supplying. I benefited especially from my earlier dealings with the merchant at the Höfdi trading post during my time on the fishing boat.

Initially the Archdeacon had been a firm believer in the curative properties of tobacco, and had received written confirmation from the renowned doctor, Professor Ole Worm of Copenhagen, of his opinion that when burning tobacco was inhaled through a pipe in the fashion of sailors, its smoke served to invigorate both the head and the chest. Professor Worm stated that this herb removed mucus in the brain and senses, *item* dried out the brain, stopped colds and runniness, and was completely harmless to those who had natural vapours.

However, the Reverend Arngrímur had come to doubt very seriously that this prescribed improvement in health was actually forthcoming, but he did not want to give up imbibing tobacco all the same, since he was completely addicted to it. The same was true of me and many others.

Spirits, on the other hand, he would serve in particular to worthy visitors and of course use to fortify himself when travelling.

I did not feel the Reverend Arngrímur devoted himself much to theology, but thought all the more eagerly about the ancient lore of the north. And once when I asked him the reason, the Archdeacon looked at me after a pause, then said, 'So you want to be a clergyman, then.'

I was lost for words, tried to show no reaction, then eventually I asked how he thought such a thing could be.

Once again Arngrímur pondered for a while, then declared his intention in the spring, when he rode over to Hólar, to request of the Bishop and keeper of the see that I be admitted to the school, if the idea did not displease me. And when I asked him how I could possibly have time off from the lambing season to let their lordships test my knowledge, he laughed and said that his word alone would suffice. His kinsman Thorlákur Skúlason the Bishop owed him that much of a favour.

The good Archdeacon was hardly exaggerating there, because the Bishop had Arngrímur to thank for his office more than anything else. What had happened was that a synod was held at Flugumýri in 1627 after Bishop Gudbrandur's death, where the clergymen were unanimous in wanting to ask Arngrímur to become Bishop, which he had in effect been for the past few years anyway and which was Gudbrandur's own stated wish while he was still capable of stating it. But Arngrímur demurred and began excusing himself such high office, although his modesty was far from ingenuous; he merely used this as a ploy to strengthen his position against the clerics in his prospective episcopal tasks, if he could continually remind them of the great reluctance with which he had finally agreed to accept this imposition.

But then what he had never reckoned with actually happened: the clergy took him exactly at his word, accepted his apologies and promptly elected Thorlákur Bishop. There were two main reasons: they thought they could tell that he would be far more manageable as a much younger and less experienced man than Arngrímur, but also a power struggle was taking place among Bishop Gudbrandur's descendants. The late Bishop's daughter Halldóra, who had managed the See during her father's illness, aimed to strengthen her position against that of her sister Kristín's husband, Sheriff Ari from Ögur, a powerful figure from the West Fjords who felt that he had more claim to control that territory. Doubtless Mistress Halldóra felt she had a suitable instrument for promoting her own cause in her illegitimate nephew Thorlákur, who had been brought up largely under her wing at the See.

That spring Arngrímur made his journey to Hólar and stayed there for some time, arranging various matters. When he returned he brought me the news that, through the word he had put in, I had been accepted into the school immediately, and that their lordships there had no more need to bother themselves about me, since his statement about my abilities had been considered valid.

33

My heart took a huge leap for joy at this news, but a hint of desperation also came over me. As the Reverend Arngrímur surely knew, neither I nor my parents had the slightest chance of paying for my schooling. My profits from dealing in tobacco and spirits would only go a fraction of the way, since they were virtually all taken out in kind. I feared, and not for the last time, that the good fortune I had within reach would slip my grasp. But that fear was soon allayed with the Archdeacon's next words, about how he himself had arranged for me to be admitted to the school as an almsboy, namely at the expense of the authorities.

So the path ahead seemed to be clear, but first I had to explain this scheme to my parents and make sure that at least they did not greatly disfavour my plans.

A few nights later I strolled over to Bjarg, told them this great news and met an almost encouraging response, in truth a better one than I had dared to hope. Admittedly my father expressed his doubts that either I or they would benefit from such a scheme, and his serious anxiety about what would become of my mother, left without a bread-winner if he were to die, which was not unlikely on account of his poor health. She would have to call someone in from outside the family then, or would be thrown off the farm and forced to beg. But my mother settled the matter herself. Said she was ready to let anything happen to her if God so willed it, in the sweet hope of eventually finding a corner of my house to stay in with me when I had become a well-off clergyman, perhaps even an archdeacon.

ow that I am left here with my affairs in such a state of
uncertainty, I must surely ask once again whether what I saw
then as my greatest stroke of luck actually turned out to be the worst
of misfortunes. I mean by being admitted to the school. There is little
point in pondering what would have happened instead of what
actually did. I cannot help recalling old Sveinn's words: 'Since God
chose to have it that way, no one can change it.'

And again a verse from my own *Ballad of Perseus* comes to mind:

> This proverb carries truth, I own,
> though many may lament it:
> Providence you can postpone
> but never once prevent it.

And in fact it was not my stay at the school in itself that led to my
misfortune, but rather meeting people there who envied and disliked
me and have consistently blocked my path ever since. I would hardly
have managed to lead my life without that kind of setback, even if I
had not gained an education. And I already had a love of scholarship
before I went to the school, and have never abandoned it. Perhaps I
would have turned out not unlike my friend Björn Jónsson from
Skardsá, a farmer but also an indefatigable scribe of ancient lore. But
scarcely with his kind of temperament, which allowed him to sit
endlessly like a pliable servant at the See, continually writing things
down for Bishop Thorlákur and praising him exuberantly in the
prefaces to many of his works.

I think I might, in my own way, have resembled more Jón Gudmundsson the Learned, who was a painter and carver in horn, wise enough but continually in trouble for his recalcitrance, and who was always driving his horns into the wall wherever he went along life's narrow alleyways. In the end he was sentenced to exile from Iceland for his sorcery, but no one would transport him out of the country and he was last said to be living on the little island of Papey off the east coast. He must still be there, if he is alive.

I met Jón, as it happens, at Melstadur around the same autumn that I started school. He was begging his way around the country then, having been sentenced at Bessastadir in 1631 after confessing to using and teaching magic signs. He had gone to Melstadur to meet the Reverend Arngrímur and I came across them sitting in the attic study above the church, deep in conversation about runes and Eddic poetry and other ancient lore. From his clothing and air I could tell that this was no man of high standing, but took him to be some degenerate clergyman, probably an old schoolfriend of the Archdeacon. That notion took even firmer root when the only thing Arngrímur would tell me about him was that they shared a nickname, and that this striking old character was also known as 'the Learned'.

But when I asked whether they were schoolfriends, they both laughed, and Arngrímur said no, but his companion said that in a sense this was true, since Arngrímur, he said, had been schooled by 'his self', while he had been schooled by 'his elf'.

I could not make head nor tail of this until the old man left and Arngrímur told me that this was a man of his own age, the infamous Jón Gudmundsson the Learned. It would not be long before the authorities sent word to sheriffs throughout Iceland to seize Jón wherever he might be found, to enforce the sentence of outlawry on him. But Jón turned the tables on them by going abroad himself at once, and there he made friends with the learned Doctor Ole Worm who, impressed with his knowledge of runes and Eddic poetry, took him under his aegis. But this did not satisfy Jón for ever. He returned to Iceland in 1637 and was sentenced again to lifelong exile from all the King's lands, but could not get a passage, and eventually the charges against him lapsed.

Do I think of this now because I shall soon follow the same course and a sentence of exile awaits me too?

In other respects I share few similarities with Jón. He has always had a Papist turn of mind and that is the origin of the sorcery in which he firmly trusts and believes, while I am repelled by Papists, their penances and hawking of pardons. I do not believe in the magic arts either, but at Melstadur it seemed convenient to have people believe I knew a thing or two – which had proved its worth when I worked with fishermen.

During my first winter with Arngrímur his grandson was staying there too, studying in preparation for the school as he had for several winters previously – Páll, whose mother was Helga, Arngrímur's daughter by his first marriage; his father was the sheriff Björn, son of Magnús from Baer and grandson of Jón the Elegant. Páll was a very young lad but extremely sharp-witted and a precocious reader. This made him somewhat arrogant and he would sometimes show that he despised me thoroughly, which I disliked but had no reply to until I discovered that Páll had a pathological fear of sorcery and sorcerers and would go wild with terror if he as much as sensed their presence. So I carefully but firmly instilled in him the idea of how skilled I was at such arts, but did so dextrously enough that he dared not mention it to anyone, for fear of me. Thus I kept little Páll tame and for a while had him eating out of the palm of my hand.

That autumn in 1634 I was not heading off to be taught by my elf as Jón the Learned had pretended to do in his youth; rather, I was soon making my way from my home at Bjarg to educate myself at Hólar cathedral school, on foot because there was no chance of providing me with a horse, and I travelled by night and by day, lying down to rest in outhouses but hardly stopping until I reached Hjaltadalur valley. It did not unfold before me in a grand panorama, any more than it did for anyone else, because the Hrísháls ridge blocked the view. But when I reached the top of the ridge, having threaded a track the whole way, before me in the tranquillity of autumn stood the great See of Hólar, which I had never set my eyes on before. Everything was exactly as Arngrímur had described the approach to it: I could see mountains towering in the distance and thought I could identify the peak called Hólabyrda, looming over the See. By squinting I could vaguely make out a cluster of buildings at its foot, and started thinking almost out loud: This is where it will happen, from here my path shall lie towards the heights of scholarly advancement. I was dizzy and felt a sensation of rejoicing shoot through me, the feeling that sometimes makes me seem to walk on air and gives me a momentary overwhelming conviction that I can do anything and will eventually know and understand all things.

Standing there in a trance, I was on the verge of bursting into song on that glorious autumn day when I suddenly realized I was not alone. The noise of a nose being blown rent the calmness and pulled me mercilessly out of my dreams and straight back down to earth. I could see a tall young man leaning up against a big rock not far from the track, with his bay horse nibbling couch grass not far away. He scrutinized his rose-coloured checked handkerchief before tucking it under his shirtsleeve and looking up. Then he seemed to notice me for the first time, and raised his arm in a friendly wave, as if we knew each other. I went over and returned his greeting.

Einar Arnfinnsson here, the young man said, offering a handshake. I knew at once that he was heading for the school from the Húnavatn district like me, and was the son of Arnfinnur Sigurdsson, the Archdeacon of Stadur in Hrutafjördur. Once long ago I had caught a glance of him, but I knew him only by reputation; he had spent two or three years at the Hólar school.

'My name's Gudmundur . . .', with something like this I started speaking to him, but got no further because Einar interrupted with a loud laugh and added, 'Andrésson from Bjarg in Midfjördur, I presume, Grettir the Strong reincarnate, eh?'

Then he started laughing even louder, presumably when he saw the look of aston ishment that I could tell came over my face.

'I mean for your accomplishments,' he continued. 'I understand from our learned friend the Archdeacon of Melstadur that such an accomplished Latin scholar has rarely entered the Hólar school as a novice.'

38

He rambled on like this for a while, then added by way of explanation that he had spent one night at Melstadur on his way east from Hrútafjördur, seen Arngrímur the Learned there and delivered his father's greetings, just at the time I left. He had expected to run into me earlier.

At first I was unsure how to take this rigmarole. Was it mockery or praise? If he was making fun of me I saw that I definitely needed to be able to answer him well, quick off the mark, snap back in the habit I had acquired on the fishing boat. I knew that he was an infamous womanizer, this Einar. Women were attracted to him and he knew how to take advantage of it. There were stories about him; his philandering had almost brought him down on more than one occasion and in fact it was one such incident, and not a pretty one, that had allegedly led to his being removed to another part of the country for a while until the trouble blew over.

I searched my mind for material for a suitable cutting remark that I could toss out at him to teach him to keep his distance. But while I was pondering, didn't Einar produce his snuffbox and offer me a pinch from it, as easy going and friendly as they come? And then I thought to myself that he could hardly be doing this to rile me. It was out of the question that he could be taking a prod at my age, so much older himself that he must have been an even more elderly novice than I was. In fact it was extraordinary for an archdeacon's son to be at school at such a late age, and a comment to this effect was on the tip of my tongue when he suddenly came across so magnanimous.

Instead, I accepted a pinch of snuff from his box as he took one for himself with great ceremony. I opened my mouth when the tobacco delivered its punch, felt myself glowing within and took a look over towards Hólar in this moment of enlightenment. At that very moment the clouds parted and the place was bathed in the glow of the sun. I stood admiring the sight in a kind of trance, and Einar stood by my side and watched it with me for a while, then started to tell me about it.

'There you have the church, of course,' he said, 'and the See itself beside it. Then, like a hillock in front of it, just like a little farmhouse standing by itself, that's the school, and at the far end of the church you can just make out the old timber building called Audunarstofa, that's where we eat.'

He went on informing me about everything as we strolled at a leisurely pace along the remainder of the track to Hólar. He explained the layout of the buildings in detail and told me about everything inside there, great and small. He pointed out what to avoid when dealing with the Bishop and his family, and he described them all, the court that ran everything at the See, the descendants of the late Bishop Gudbrandur Thorláksson. He told me about every single person to be found there, the headmaster and the teacher or *Locatus*, as he called him, and the steward of the See and the vicar of the church, all the way down to the stable boys and serving girls.

Behind him he reined in the horse which now carried both his and my belongings. And just as we were entering the yard, we made a pact that he would be my *tutor*, as he informed me that the older boys who supervised the younger ones were called.

$\mathfrak{I}$n his *Golden Ass* or *Metamorphoses*, the only book I have to keep myself amused here in my prison, Lucius, who is supposed to be the author Lucius Apuleius himself, gives an account of the terrible situation he found himself in after being transformed, by a tragic mistake, into an ass while he was in Hypata as the guest of Milo and Pamphile. His metamorphosis began when the wondrously beautiful Fotis, his mistress and a servant of the old hag Pamphile, told him about her lady's practice of turning herself by magic into whatever type of animal she chose. Maddened with excitement, Lucius insisted on seeing the old woman performing this act, and when the chance arose he persuaded Fotis to conceal him where he watched Pamphile undress, smear her body with oils and pronounce spells. Thereupon she began to transform and sprouted feathers, wings, a beak and talons, until she had turned into a perfect owl and finally took wing and flew out of the house. She was expected back in the evening, when it was Fotis' duty to wait for her with a special potion of dill and laurel ready for the old woman to drink, which neutralized the effect of the fluid within her so that she assumed her old, sorry state.

Having seen and learned all this, Lucius became enflamed with such a burning passion to be able to turn into a bird himself, that he did not give up until Fotis, trembling, managed to steal a phial of ointment for him from her lady's casket. He then repeated the old woman's procedure, stripped off his clothes, smeared himself from top to toe and started flapping his arms at once in order to fly into the air.

But this time the outcome was completely different, as often befalls the devisers of trickery. No feathers sprouted forth and he felt no wings growing, but instead he could feel his hair turning wiry and his soft skin toughening into hide. His fingers and toes bunched together into hoofs, and a tail grew from his rear. His face was swelled, his mouth spread, his nostrils flared and his lips went flabby. In the end he realized that he had not turned into a bird, but was a plain ass.

Then the beautiful Fotis wept at the top of her voice, lamenting her haste, for she had clearly taken the wrong box from the casket. And when the good Lucius was about to accuse her of what may be called making an ass of him, he found to his great tribulation that he had also completely lost the power of human speech and deportment, and could do nothing other than stare at the light-hearted wench with his drooping lips and moist donkey's eyes in speechless accusation.

But Fotis told him not to despair, because to turn back to his former shape he needed only to eat a few roses which she said she would provide for him the next day.

But it did not turn out that way. To avoid further trouble, Lucius decided to spend the night in a stable with his own horse and one of the donkeys from the place where he was staying, but was harshly persecuted by them, and when he tried to defend himself a stable boy came over to thrash him. Fortunately for Lucius, sooner rather than later, some thieves broke into Milo's house at just that moment and the stable boy fled, but without a moment's hesitation the robbers seized the ass that Lucius had become, loaded their loot on to him and took him away with them. With this the hero's ordeals began, and in the book he relates much of what he suffered, although he was always driven by the hope that eventually he would find the posy of roses that might endow him with human shape anew.

Have I perhaps met the same fate as Lucius? Am I one of the unfledged who would be a bird, wise as an owl and soaring high, but am forced to sit here in this place like an ass tethered to a stall? That may be, but where then are the roses to be found that I might eat and become myself anew? And who is myself? Am I the one I was?

Metamorphosis, at any rate, was what I hoped would happen to me at Hólar. As soon as we entered the yard at that great place I felt that I had already achieved considerable respect. Both because I perhaps started to swell at the splendid buildings I beheld and could rightly regard as my own home, and no less because I felt straightaway that I benefited from my new-found friendship with the Archdeacon's lively son, Einar Arnfinnsson. We had hardly arrived before I realized that Einar had to be exceptionally popular there. I relished bathing myself in his glory and assumed at first that it was no small stroke of luck to be able to make my entrance there in his company.

Einar immediately began delivering greetings left and right to the people who worked at the See, with playful banter and jokes. The farmhands looked up from their tasks and gladly returned his greetings, children flocked around him, playing and laughing. Bashful serving maids waved to him from all over the place, giggling and whispering, some gave meaningful smiles and others stared at him seriously with yearning and passion in their dark eyes, others still burst into tears and ran away sobbing, hiding their faces in their aprons.

Beneath a wall stood a group of schoolboys whom he greeted heartily, kissing many of them and addressing them by name, patting shoulders everywhere. He always had something specific to say to each one, while they all greeted him warmly in return.

Had I expected the same respect from my prospective school-fellows to devolve effortlessly upon me through his glory, then I was seriously mistaken, because it was apparent at once their attitude towards me was different. Einar had not even managed to tell them my name or anything else about me before their mockery began pouring down upon me.

'What little squirt have you got there with you? Your private *famulus* from Hrútafjördur?' These were the words of a stout, acne-faced teenager whose voice kept breaking. He was laughing in a loud voice, highly impressed by his own humour, and the whole chorus joined in.

Einar shared one roar with them, like a polite commiseration with those louts, then turned serious, told them to play it down and then launched into a great eulogy of my merits. The accomplishments that graced my person few people were endowed with, he said, unimposing

43

a figure though I might be. They would do well to bear in mind that the qualities considered most worthwhile at seats of learning were not measured in ells from the nose downwards, but rather in inches from the nose upwards, more to the point in interior inches rather than exterior ones. The lads were somewhat quelled by this news, some of them looked at me in wonder and disbelief. There was even a hint of something approaching a token of respect on the occasional face. Then a child's bright voice blared out from the middle of the group.

'Everyone's accomplished in his own way. As far as I can see, that's my grandfather's farmhand.'

I recognized the voice and saw that its owner was none other than little Páll Björnsson, the Reverend Arngrímur's grandson, who was now beginning his third year at Hólar in spite of his tender age. He seemed to have toughened up a fair amount since we met at Melstadur before and had probably conquered his fear of sorcery.

At this, the laughter burst out again and destroyed the impact that Einar's speech had made. The fat lad led the proceedings, pulling faces and fooling around, until Einar scolded him. They all called him Thorkell, and I realized that this was the son of Gudmundur Hákonarson, the Sheriff of Thingeyrar, and thereby the legitimate off-spring of the Hólar dynasty on his mother's side, since his mother was Halldóra, the daughter of Ari from Ögur and his wife Kristín, who was the daughter of Bishop Gudbrandur.

Though I felt like tearing them all off a strip for their rude behaviour towards a stranger, I remembered Einar's words about paying deference to the court, and managed to control myself despite the lampoons that were tickling my tongue. But I shouldered a grudge against them after I had settled in better. I took an immediate dislike to the gang. They were all clearly the sons of high-ranking men, and felt very self-important for it. This was like a foretaste of the adversity I have had to face ever since. All I could hope was that I would be better accepted by the alms boys.

Instead of answering back I pulled Einar aside and told my new friend in a low voice that I wanted to go straight to see the Bishop and deliver a greeting from the Reverend Arngrímur, announcing my arrival at the same time, as the learned Archdeacon had advised me.

'That's more like it,' Einar laughed, 'that's what I like to see. Don't be awed by rank if you want to get ahead, that's for sure.' But perhaps there was no urgency, he said, because the Bishop would be hardly out of bed so early in the day, besides which I had as much business to see the Rector or *Locatus* to begin with.

I said I wanted to follow to the letter the instructions that my great mentor the Reverend Arngrímur had given me. And one of them had been always to take my matters to the highest authority and not waste my breath on underlings. Einar grinned, led me between the buildings and pointed out the Bishop's residence, an elegant house in the middle of the cluster. He said he was going to the kitchen to see a few of his 'sweethearts', as he called them, check out those returning after the summer and inspect the new material.

He headed off there while I put down my bags against the wall of the house, knocked on the door and entered the passage leading to another house, the one Einar had pointed out to me. I called down the passage then knocked once again, at the door to the house itself, several times until a grumpy serving girl eventually shambled up to answer. She looked at me with an expression of disbelief, then said that the Lord Bishop was still eating.

I replied that I was in no hurry, I could sit down and wait there if she would just let him know that Gudmundur Andrésson, the special disciple of Arngrímur the Learned, Archdeacon of Melstadur in Hrútafjördur, was present in person. She gave me a strange look and then pottered back inside, and when she did not return I assumed that I had been granted an audience, since otherwise she would probably have come straight back to turn me away or announce the time of an appointment.

Almost half an hour later she came back out, told me to follow her and went outdoors. There she pointed to a building she called the New House, which was annexed to the Bishop's residence and used by him as a study. The girl told me that Bishop Thorlákur was ready to see me there.

I immediately sensed some surprise and curiosity on the Bishop's part when I stepped in after knocking, and entered the room when told to do so. The Bishop was sitting at his desk over some papers, a man in his thirties at a guess, with well-proportioned features and portly but with a slightly deathly look on his face. I greeted him as respectfully as I knew, and delivered a warm greeting from the Reverend Arngrímur.

It must be said that, unlike what would happen later, Bishop Thorlákur was not unfriendly to me at first. After several enquiries about Arngrímur's health he mentioned that everything to do with my schooling could be handled by the Headmaster and Steward. They had been informed that I should enjoy full alms and everything had been arranged. Now I should prove that I deserved this great privilege. Nor did I need to take any examination, since they had complete faith in Arngrímur's testimony about my knowledge of Latin and the other compulsory subjects, he said, and it was to be hoped that I would not cause the Archdeacon's word to be doubted. My further advancement was hereby in my own hands. These were his very words, that I was the master of my own fortune. Thus spake the architect of my misfortune!

he more wretched that my life has become in my confinement, the more often I think back to the amusing misconception of which I was at first possessed, thinking I could stride right into the King's palace to a splendid welcome, as if I expected him to take me straight into his court and make me his right-hand man. Little has come true in that respect, however, and I hardly mourn it. But the most appalling thing is never hearing what people plan to do with me. The more that the cold, hardship and hunger oppress me, the more I feel I would welcome and be cheered by anything whatsoever. Even the news that I was to be sent to Bremerholm prison for the rest of my life, which would not be long anyway, or simply executed. When the guards fill me and empty me, I mean my food trough and chamberpot, I continually try to ask them if there is any news, but they always shrug or launch into long, fast speeches that I have trouble understanding.

My main source of news is Fredrik the murderer. He was sentenced to death two years ago, but the widow of the man he beat to death either cannot or will not pay the executioner's fee, finding it cheaper to pay for his food in the tower; not surprisingly, she keeps the rations slender. Fredrik says that she really ought to be thankful to him for ridding her of her husband, who was absolute scum.

The murderer accepts plenty of morsels from me when I am too weak to hold anything down, which sometimes happens, and continually informs me about how things work in here. I find it increasingly easy to understand his speech as time goes by. I have asked him to supply me with some paper and a pen so that I can write to the King himself, the Archbishop or my travelling companion Governor Bjelke to ask for my case to be considered, or to someone of importance in this city who might be able to help me.

Fredrik says this will be no problem as soon as I can pay for it, but then I ask him how he thinks I can get any money all the while I am sitting here. He counters by asking whether I have any supporters up there in the cold land of ice who could send me anything.

I am forced to vest my hopes in the arrival of the autumn ship soon, and that one of my friends, having guessed my fate, will have had the sense to send me something that might be of help before I drop down dead. Meanwhile, Fredrik the murderer has taken pity on me and given me a few scraps of paper, an apology for a pen and a dash of ink. I have tried writing to Governor Bjelke and Bishop Brochmand of Zealand, twice in fact, but have received no reply.

The thought often occurs to me that our present King is not a man of great character and my situation would have been completely different were his renowned father Christian IV still alive.

It is often the case with great men, that their descendants prove to be small, and all the smaller the more they try to stretch and crane themselves to the stature of their begetters. I found this out myself with a different court at a different time in a different country, namely at Hólar. The custom there was to prefer kinsman and friends, often with horrendous results, although I cannot tar them all with the same brush.

Bishop Thorlákur Skúlason, who proved worst of all to me when I needed him most, was one such crown prince: grandson of the all-encompassing Bishop Gudbrandur and son of the Bishop's illegitimate daughter Steinunn and her husband Skúli Einarsson from Svartár-dalur. He had been brought up with his grandfather at Hólar, tied to the apron strings of Mistress Halldóra Gudbrandsdóttir who controlled everything she cared to there and played no small part in Thorlákur's being preferred to Arngrímur during the episcopal election.

Thorlákur had just turned thirty when he was awarded the title of Bishop in 1628 and had sat in that seat of honour for six years when I arrived at Hólar. But after he was Bishop he was tormented by a powerful yearning to make himself famous with a great deed that would be compared to his grandfather's achievements. So he opted to do the same as his old grandfather, publish the Bible, but undertook the task in a frightful hurry. He tinkered away at this all the while I was at Hólar, preoccupied with printing the new Bible translation which he thought would make him immortal. He had translated the Holy Book himself from the Danish and in many ways suffered for it, since learned men made fun of his work and it was sometimes even said he must have thought God Himself was Danish.

The Bishop had married Kristín, daughter of the Lawspeaker Gísli Hákonarson, four years before I turned up there, so their children were still young and others were born during my school years.

Apart from Mistress Halldóra, who despite lifelong spinsterhood had become a kind of materfamilias of the whole place, the relatives included Headmaster Vigfús Árnason himself, who was married to the Bishop's sister and was therefore his brother-in-law, and a new Keeper of the See or Steward, Benedikt Pálsson, Bishop Gudbrandur's grandson. The family roll-call went right on down to the old duffer Pétur Gudmundsson, who was bellringer and errand-runner and closely related to Gudbrandur. These last two, Benedikt and Pétur, were in fact fine men in most respects, became my friends and even put in a good word for me later when I clashed with the Bishop. Benedikt in particular showed good will towards me and tried to help me later when he was King's Agent at Möðruvellir cloister. He was a solid character, trained as a barber with the Germans in Hamburg and had many remarkable stories to tell from the time when Turkish pirates captured him on board one of the Hamburg vessels and took him to Barbary as a hostage until his relatives paid the ransom and he went to Hólar.

These high-born relatives enjoyed great support from each other, and their nepotism was fair enough when decent people happened to be involved, but a bad thing if they were bad. Anyone who breached the discipline required to maintain that order was mercilessly punished. This had happened with Pétur the bellringer's son, Hallgrímur, who had been brought up at Hólar and had every door open to him. But he had disobeyed Bishop Gudbrandur's discipline and composed some scurrilous lampoons about him and Arngrímur the Learned, was expelled and set off as an adventurer abroad, until Bishop Brynjólfur of Skálholt ran into him and sent him to school in Copenhagen. Towards the end of my time at the school, word came back that Hallgrímur had fallen into adultery with a married Icelandic woman who had turned unashamedly heathen after long captivity with the Turks; she was one of a group of released hostages who had reached Copenhagen and he was supposed to teach the scriptures. Or, as they say, instead of spiritual knowledge he gave her carnal knowledge. When this came to light his relatives in the north lost no time in condemning him and turning their noses up at him, with the sole exception of his poor father. Hallgrímur did legally marry the same woman later and I got to know them well when I started going south to buy fish after I had returned to Bjarg.

The best thing that could be said about Bishop Thorlákur was that he was a true friend of scholarship in spite of everything. He saw to it that Björn Jónsson from Skardsá was able to spend long periods at Hólar in pursuit of scholarship, writing many of his works and chronicles there. Björn, who soon became a close friend of mine, was also a great poet, always composing verses, including some sharp ones against the Great Edict, on the strength of which I later presumed that I would be allowed to protest against the same ruling. One of his poems contains the memorable barb:

> Now it will cost you a fine
> like theft and other crime,
> the Great Edict deprives
> men of their goods and their lives.
> But the love of women is human all the time.

Another visitor to Hólar was the person dearest of all to me, even though she was related to the Bishop, the woman whose love I humanly wanted, Sigrídur Jónsdóttir. My dear Sigga from Stadarbakki. Examining and reflecting here on the lot I received instead of what I sought, it is almost amusing to think that less than a decade has passed since I seriously imagined that she could be mine.

We had known each other for a long time and I had always been in love with her from a distance, and sometimes let myself dream about it in absolute hopelessness. Yet I could only assume that she was fond of me too, because she was always kind and friendly towards me even though she was considered of higher rank.

She was three years my junior and I first saw her at a church service at Stadarbakki. Later our paths sometimes crossed while we were watching over flocks of lambs and I often told her stories, various things old Sveinn had taught me, and she always told me how interesting I was.

She was the daughter of Arngrímur the Learned's sister. Her mother was Gudrún Jónsdóttir, the wife of the Reverend Gissur Gamlason from Stadarbakki, who had fallen into temptation when she was young and unmarried and had Sigrídur by the Reverend Jón Oddsson. It was on account of this kinship that she went to Melstadur, where she came during my final winter there to help Arngrímur's wife to look after all their children. We were still on good terms there, although nothing was said and no promises were made, such things being outside the boundaries that I knew I had been set.

Then she happened to come to Hólar a year after me, to learn handicrafts from Mistress Halldóra. At first she had few friends and felt lonely, and so she sought my company to some extent because she knew me already, although she was not expected to mix much with the schoolboys. She was always very friendly towards me and provided me with some good things after she started finding her way about. I could tell that she kept a close watch on me and cared for my well-being, showing genuine happiness at my increasing academic success and shared my pain if I was treated unjustly, when she would try to seek redress.

However, nothing was ever discussed between us and still neither of us promised the other anything. There could not have been any hope of that. The only thing was that I asked my good friend Einar Arnfinnsson, and made him swear a solemn promise, never to lay a finger on Sigrídur on his nocturnal journeys.

From our entire acquaintance I felt I could conclude that Sigrídur would not be entirely averse to me, so I set my mind upon asking for her hand at some time in the future.

On the evening of my first day at school, I had to go through the initiation ceremonies that the boys inflict on the new arrivals in order to belittle and humble them. The few of us who were starting then were made to 'walk fire', as it was called. This involves the older boys sitting down in two rows facing each other, with their legs stretched out so that their heels touch. Then the newcomer is blindfolded and made to walk or run between the rows. A great fray ensues, with legs flying everywhere kicking at the novice, so the course is tough to run and generally costs a tumble or two. However, bad falls or serious injuries rarely result, since two of the older boys are supposed to stand behind the rows and lead the novice by the hands through the ordeal. But when it was my turn, halfway through the fire the boys who were holding my hands suddenly let go and started jostling me, while the ones on the floor kicked me all the harder, so I lost my footing and took a bad fall against one of the beds, leaving a pain in my ribcage for some time afterwards. I was harangued too, and the commotion stopped only when my friend and tutor Einar arrived on the scene, told them this was unfair play and ordered them to stop at once. They spared me more rough treatment for the time being, but from this I should have concluded that my later enemies and accusers would not flinch at tripping me up if they felt my path forward was too easy.

In spite of several early clashes I was quick to find my feet at Hólar. I was well equipped with my solid studies at the feet of the Reverend Arngrímur at Melstadur, and I also devoted myself eagerly, even zealously, to my studies, sometimes even falling asleep in my clothes over my books. During my time at Hólar, which turned out to be only four years, I moved rapidly up through the classes. In my second autumn I was top of the lower class and went straight up from there to the upper class in the third autumn.

I was the last person to boast or swell up with an excess of ambition in front of the others, whatever I might have thought. I found nothing remarkable about being the equal of anyone in the lower class, since I was older than them and had had what could be called a solid grounding. Most of them were scarcely out of their infancy, all the sons of clergymen and important people, and many were set to be educated more from compulsion than special talents or interest; some snivelled in the evenings, wet their beds every night and called out for their mothers in their sleep. I, on the other hand, was a fully grown man, experienced and hardened by various of life's labours and driven by the sharp, grabbing ambition of the pauper who suddenly finds himself given a chance.

But the old proverb soon came true, that one man's cheer is another man's fear; namely quite a few lads in the lower class objected to the fact that such a low-born and poor pupil should soar past them without hindrance, and they saw it as an insult that a person such as I should tower above them. Therefore I soon made sworn enemies and enviers who never let a chance go by, then or later, to slur and humiliate me, although generally they gained nothing by it since I remained unbudged and answered all their abuse in kind, which in turn irritated them even more. Einar stood firmly behind me, too, which kept them at bay for some time. In other respects I had little to do with them and absorbed myself all the more deeply in my studies, which served only to magnify their grumbling and their urges to torment me even more.

The ringleader in baiting me was Thorkell, son of Sheriff Gudmundur Hákonarson from Thingeyrar, the one who had showered me with the most abuse on my first day. He intensified his campaign in my second autumn when I had already easily surpassed him, and others too who had many years of schooling behind them. Of course, it was not exactly a major achievement to outstrip such oafs, most of whom lacked the slightest aptitude for learning from books. Thorkell was a giant for his age, strong as an ox, fat and big-arsed just like his father. He kept a circle of younger lads around him, who admired him and for whom he had to play his role to the hilt. Admittedly he could show his better side if these imps of his were not around, but this was rare because they used to go around in a gang. In particular he used the boys to wait on him and keep him informed of gossip and complaints. Thorkell and his little devils did not manage to pull any tricks on me for the first years, when I could shelter behind Einar. But not for lack of wanting to.

Páll Björnsson followed Thorkell and his gang around everywhere, but unlike them he was a clever student. He had played his part in the assault on me when I arrive at the school, but I knew from the past how to keep clear of him. I soon gained control over him by scaring him once again with my alleged sorcery, and it emerged that despite his boastfulness in front of the other schoolboys he still feared it more than anything else. Once I showed him in confidence some pages of runes, which I made sure of burning before they came to anyone else's notice. I hinted to little Páll about various tortures that might be in store for him if he incited my wrath any more. I also pretended to have found out all about the old book of magic which was kept in a secret place in the school out of the reach of the authorities. All this led him to keep himself in check and even try to soften Thorkell in his vehemence towards me. This trick worked well for the time being, but would later rebound on me.

The cold feelings and hatred that Bishop Thorlákur bore towards me as time went by originated in a series of embarrassingly trivial incidents at Hólar during my school years. There the seeds were planted that would later sprout so mightily and finally burst into bloom with my imprisonment.

The aforementioned louts whom I surpassed in class finally came to bear right down upon me when my friend and advocate Einar Arnfinnsson left Hólar after matriculating during my second spring at the school. For the most part these were childish pranks and scuffles that I brushed off like flies, knowing that anger is the reward of its provoker. As usual, Thorkell Gudmundsson was the ringleader against me. My main weapon against those devils was to deliver scorching lampoons about them when I felt their pranks had gone too far – such as the time when Thorkell and one of his followers and relatives by the name of Magnús pissed on my mattress, forcing me to approach the Steward for some new hay to stuff it with, which the good Benedikt willingly provided. Without witnesses, I could not invite punishment on those rogues for their foul prank; that was the low trick they always used. But my lampoon about the incident was soon on everyone's lips at Hólar, and brought many a smile:

> They did their tricks with rampant dicks
> upon the dripping mattress.
> But the only juice they could produce
> was half a cup of cat piss.

This helped to take the wind out their sails for a while and they backed off, but their hatred and vindictiveness towards me simmered and grew – as would soon emerge.

Towards the spring of my third year, it was announced that three of Mistress Halldóra Gudbrandsdóttir's silver spoons had gone missing.

These were great treasures, and it was strongly suspected that one of the pupils was responsible for their disappearance. Action was quickly taken, the whole school was searched and all the boys were ordered to be present while this was done. The highest authorities of the school and the See were there, namely the Bishop himself and his Steward, along with the Vicar of the church, the Headmaster and *Locatus*. Their Lordships stormed through our dormitory turning over mattresses and covers and peering into nooks and crannies, and plenty of things came to light, but no spoons anywhere.

Then the Bishop ordered a search of all our trunks, and we were told to hand over the keys. So they went from one trunk to the next, rummaging and rooting around inside them, but still failed to find the silver. While all this was going on I sat on my bed, completely unafraid of course, since I knew myself to be innocent, absolutely unaware that a trick had been played on me. I could not believe any person capable of such base behaviour, even though I understand I am not thought particularly well disposed towards others.

Without hesitation I handed over the key to my humble trunk where there was nothing to be found but my sorry clothes and a few dried fish besides my books, paper and pens, and I said that by all means they should search my things; this was only right and natural. Benedikt began rummaging around there, while Bishop Thorlákur peered inside to watch.

And then when the Steward happened to pull out some brown woollen socks and lift them up, the coveted spoons tumbled out. Everyone inside was struck dumb, and I leapt to my feet saying in the humblest of words that this must be a trick, the spoons were nothing to do with me and someone must have planted them there as a practical joke to get me into trouble.

Bishop Thorlákur swelled with rage, snatched the spoons up and asked me in a trembling voice as he began beating me over the head with them, 'What's this then, you rogue? Is this the way the alms boy repays charity? Not only do you shamelessly deny what has clearly been proved, but you also make false accusations about your innocent schoolmates. But there are plenty of witnesses here.'

He capped this by slapping me around the face and screamed as if deranged that I was expelled from the school and ought to crawl away at once, but would not get off that lightly – he wanted the authorities of the See to meet about how to punish me for my 'criminal act', as he called it. This was a clear case of theft, and there was nothing for it but to report the matter to the Sheriff.

I was thunderstruck to see the Bishop so mad with rage, because normally he never showed the slightest change of expression. Later I heard that just before they searched us, his printer had dropped the galley holding two pages of his Bible translation. Then he stormed out, after ordering Benedikt to keep me prisoner in one of the sheds, which that good man was forced to do, though he had tears in his eyes for my sake.

So there I was behind lock and key for the first time in my life, though not the last, as it has turned out. My stay there, however, did not last long, because immediately the next morning Benedikt came in, woke me up and told me to go back to the school and continue my studies as if nothing had happened, because the matter was over. I did so, and it was only later that day that I heard from the *Locatus*, when I pressed him to answer, exactly what had happened, why my fortunes had taken such a turn once again.

What had happened was that the same evening my dear Sigrídur could tell from some unguarded words spoken by Gísli, the Bishop's son, that he knew something about the disappearance of the spoons. She informed Mistress Halldóra, having difficulty in making her point at first because the spinster reacted wildly and said it was scandalous of me to stoop so low as to take advantage of an innocent child to do my evil deed. She grilled the boy to explain the matter, and Gísli cracked on the spot and told the whole story, which was that Thorkell and his obedient servant Magnús had tricked Gísli into pilfering the spoons and secretly handing them over, with the promise of some raisins and a silk neckerchief in return. Little Gísli did so but, *nota bene*, earned neither his raisins nor his kerchief. He gave away the secret because he felt himself betrayed of his reward.

All this then came to light and the matter was perfectly clear to everybody. So I was released and the Bishop apologized to me, grudgingly though, for falsely accusing me. But he added that were it not for my venomous tongue, and my arrogance and impulsiveness when I was accused of the deed, then such harsh treatment might never have been necessary. In other words: I had only myself to blame, even for the mean tricks that the boys played on me, which were supposedly the result of my lampoons, and for the Bishop's impetuous punishment of me. I said nothing, the wiser for experience, but thought all the more.

What I found worst of all was that no action was taken against Thorkell and his companion. What had been pure theft on my part changed into a harmless prank once they were implicated in it. They were ticked off in private by the Bishop, but in other respects the matter was dropped. The more I pondered this, the heavier it weighed upon me, and as on previous occasions I had no other solace than to vent my feelings in lampoons. So I composed my *Ode to the Silver Spoons*, a scurrilous poem ridiculing the Bishop's part in this incident, which includes the following verse:

> From misanthropy's damp hay
> many bundles he'll lash up,
> from the sea of accusations
> he ever hauls his fish up,
> serving poor Gvendur rations
> on to his dish up,
> kindling lamentations,
> tears and sweat, piss and hiccup.
> Time and tide, I say,
> wait for no bishop.

Oho, that I really should not have done. It is pointless to compose verses that no one hears, and I was tempted to teach them to a few people. They began to float around and reached the highest ears, and this poem would freeze the Bishop's feelings towards me so much that it may have been instrumental in the fact that he failed me in my moment of greatest need.

I did not suffer any more disturbance from the boys for the rest of that year, nor the next one, which was my last at the cathedral school. This happened automatically when some of them left the school, which they had never had any reason to attend in the first place. Thorkell's wings were clipped then and he never soared in his evil pranks once his imps had left. He too left the school in the end, several years after I had finished my studies there. None the less, Thorkell and in particular his father saw fit to claim that it was largely on my humble account that his academic career came to such a sorry end.

$\mathcal{S}$omewhere in the first book of *The Golden Ass* is an account of the remarkable behaviour of an animal called *castor*, the beaver. When pursued by hunters and dogs closing in, and it senses defeat, the beaver takes the drastic action of biting off its private parts and leaving them on the trail, in the hope that its pursuers will pause on finding them and give it more chance to escape. In the book, the sorceress Meroe is said to have exploited that animal's instinct to take revenge on one of her lovers who had betrayed her with another woman. With one of her spells she transformed her poor lover into a beaver, doubtless hoping that he would be persecuted while still in this form and resort to dismembering himself, so that he would prove inadequate for his new mistress when he returned to human shape.

Improbable as such episodes may seem, they are more likely to contain another, hidden significance: in this instance, then, presumably that the beaver's alleged behaviour may be compared to that of men who stake too much in order to avoid grim fates.

But I think that I know one man who would never adopt such a drastic course however long he would need to remain cursed in the body of a beaver, nor however hard pressed he was. This is my friend Einar Arnfinnsson. Though, it would doubtless have served my interests better had this happened to him.

Although Einar had matriculated and left Hólar, he was still not far away. He had immediately been called to the office of deacon at Reyni-stadur cloister in Skagafjördur. Our acquaintance continued, and we met up as far as our other obligations would allow. He could not help hearing about the troubles and conflicts that I had to suffer at the Episcopal See.

Once when he came there to see me at the end of my third year, he had set his mind on trying to ensure that my stay at Hólar lasted no longer than was absolutely necessary. He said he had spoken to the keeper of the cloister at Reynistadur about allowing me to stay there for the summer if I wished. There I could study energetically, and otherwise earn my keep by doing jobs on Einar's own little plot of land or at the cloister when needed. I thought this was an excellent plan.

But Einar had a further motive: he urged me to use this opportunity not only to increase my knowledge and refresh my spirit, but also to try to matriculate straightaway the following spring and thereby get away from Hólar, cocking a snook at my accusers and demanding office and wealth. I, on the other hand, saw countless obstacles to the Bishop's agreeing to send me through the school so quickly that I could finish my studies in just four years, since most people spent five or six years there or even longer. I was convinced that the Bishop would regard this as degrading for the school.

Einar told me to ignore that and leave the Bishop to worry over it for himself. He said he had already discussed the idea of broaching the subject with the Bishop with many people at the See whom he knew to be well disposed towards me. Especially the Bishop's relatives, such as his brother-in-law Headmaster Vigfús and Benedikt the Steward, not to mention Mistress Halldóra, who had never done anything in my favour despite the embarrassing episode with the silver spoons. It generally did not take much thought to work out in which direction any wheels would turn that she decided to set in motion there. It was also conceivable, as a last resort, to turn to the Reverend Arngrímur and see whether he still held any sway there.

I answered Einar that even though all those people might be well disposed towards me in their own ways, or at least not ill disposed, it was not certain that they would feel ready or bothered to launch into long disquisitions about my merits and qualities with the Bishop, knowing that he was against me.

But Einar replied with a loud laugh that the issue at stake was not necessarily my merits, adding, 'Someone might even point out to the Bishop how convenient it could be for him not to have you in front of his eyes much longer, or your venomous verses in his servants' ears.'

However it was all arranged, whoever may have said whatever to whomsoever, everything turned out as Einar had planned. I went straight to Reynistadur as soon as school broke up in the spring and spent the summer there engrossed in my studies. There was a large collection of books at the cloister which I pored over. I felt at the time that I could not imagine anything better than to be able to spend my whole life doing just that. I did not manage to take my thoughts any further, I did not even allow myself to dream of going to university.

And when I returned to the school in the autumn it was perfectly plain after the examination and perhaps after a talk by someone to someone else, that the course seemed clear for me to matriculate the following spring. I began preparing myself even more energetically than before. If I had put an effort into my studies before, then my vigour ran riot now, and was often followed by the ecstatic frenzy which I feel descending upon me when I am under pressure.

That winter passed and my studying was the only noteworthy thing that happened. I became close friends with Vigfús the schoolmaster, one result of which was that he set me the ideal text to preach upon in my matriculation sermon, namely Proverbs 25, verse 4, to wit: *Take the dross from the silver, and there shall come forth a vessel for the finer.*

I was able to transfer those words to the repentant sinner who receives God's mercy, and also gave a prayer of thanks for His mercy at having lifted me up from the dust and my humble origins. Everyone enjoyed listening to it and my preaching was highly praised. Even the Bishop himself spoke well about it, though he surely suspected that it contained some hidden meaning against him, which was not in fact the case. I matriculated with honours on the seventh day of the month of July, *anno domini* 1638.

As my friends were celebrating with me and wishing me luck and all the best at this turning-point in my life, Bishop Thorlákur also happened to come by and, unprompted, began encouraging me to continue my studies and seek admission to the university. He said he would gave me a reference without hesitation to make my entrance easier. Many people heard this, but I was so convinced that my poverty would prevent anything coming of such a venture for the time being that I did not bother to grab the chance when it was offered. I merely thanked him and said I would take up the offer if I were to go abroad. Often since I have regretted not having sought that letter of reference at once, for it soon became obvious that it would not be easy to profit from episcopal influence.

Among those who visited me was Sigrídur from Stadarbakki. As a parting gift she brought me some socks she had knitted, and then said she would miss me and implored me not to forget her now that I was a man of such great learning.

first set eyes upon Thorleifur Kortsson as I was preparing to leave the Hólar school, the day after I had matriculated from it. I had put my meagre belongings into my trunk and a fair-sized sack and had strapped them, with some other things as a counterweight, on to a packhorse that Björn from Skardsá had lent me. I was supposed to return the horse to Skardsá after transporting my belongings to Reynistadur, where I would rest. From there I expected to borrow a horse to take them back to Bjarg, which was my destination for the time being, since it did not look as if I had any other place of refuge. Perhaps my future was not quite as wide open as Einar had led me to believe during his greatest exhortations.

As I left the school building for the last time, kissing farewell to my best friends and benefactors such as Björn, Vigfús the Headmaster and Benedikt Pálsson, I noticed Thorkell Gudmundsson as he came waddling round the corner some distance away, and a lad with him, peculiar and dandyish, dressed in the foreign fashion, who was talking to Thorkell with much flapping of his arms and peculiar sibilants which buzzed and splashed from his mouth as if his head were a huge beehive. When I asked the others about him they told me he was a relative of Thorkell's and the nephew of Sheriff Gudmundur Hákonarson, by the name of Thorleifur Kortsson, a young tailor who had recently returned to Iceland after an apprenticeship in his trade in Hamburg. He had come to Hólar to sew new clothes for the Bishop, his wife and children, from cloth that the Bishop had ordered expressly for that purpose and which had been delivered on the spring cargo ship.

The two men fell silent when they reached where we were standing, but no sooner had they passed us by than they resumed their conversation. I noticed Thorkell leaning towards the tailor as they walked on, whispering something into his ear, at which his relative began to take frequent glances back at us. I felt certain that Thorkell was informing the new arrival about all my devilish deeds. Eventually I saw them stop beneath a wall not far away, where Thorkell continued to explain and his relative listened, nodded and asked questions. The last time I looked over I could feel one of his eyes fixed upon me, cold and dead and scrutinizing, while the brim of the tailor's foppish feathered hat covered the other. Have I ever been given the evil eye in the full sense of that phrase it was there and then, and strange cold shudders ran through my body.

I mentioned to my friends that with his eye and hat he could pass for the god Odin himself, to which Björn from Skardsá replied, 'You have a gift for cutting remarks, Gudmundur, but this joke is in rather poor taste. As it happens, Thorleifur had an accident in his youth which left him with only one eye. Though I doubt he is a match for Odin in any respect, except perhaps with a needle and thread.'

The others said they had heard how taciturn and self-effacing he tended to be. Part of the explanation may have been how lisping his speech had become after his long stay in Hamburg, and that he could find nothing but German words to describe many things, in particular relating to his trade.

Benedikt said he had known Thorleifur well during the years he spent in Hamburg and that he was preoccupied with sorcery and sorcerers, whom he feared greatly and regarded as the scourge of the Icelandic nation. If he could be drawn to speak on any subject, it was this. Especially if he managed to air his opinion that the Icelanders showed far too much leniency towards such scum. Not only was there not enough firewood in Iceland to burn sorcerers to ashes, but also a sorry lack of all equipment for extracting the correct confessions and appropriate recantations from them. He would name various types of tongs and screws and clamps and other devices which he knew in great detail and was particularly fascinated by. He would often launch into long speeches on the subject, producing illustrated books and catalogues by way of explanation.

I bade all my friends farewell with kisses and words of friendship, but my mind suddenly became preoccupied with Thorleifur Kortsson's evil eye as I rode away from Hólar. I felt it was that place's farewell to me, and did not bode well.

None the less I set off from there towards my parents' farm at Bjarg in good spirits, though my future was completely uncertain. For a while afterwards I felt as though I had not left Hólar shorn and fleeced, nor branded with the earmark of the See, namely by the removal of both ears. I would be branded later, when I would keep my ears, but be given an unfair hearing instead.

ere in this tower, every day I spend tends to resemble all the others and there is little in the way of noteworthy events. Sometimes, however, I am permitted to leave my cell, like Fredrik the murderer who generally goes around free inside the tower. At other times I am firmly locked away. I cannot exactly work out what it is that determines these arrangements; as far as I can tell it is largely the whims of the watchmen and their own convenience. Some of the other prisoners are able to win their favour with bribes and offerings, gifts of food and drink and even money. Nothing of the sort is at my disposal, since I am destitute and not well enough supplied with food by the authorities anyway to have anything left over; nor am I certain that any watchman would be such a wretch as to desire to share it with me were it offered. Besides, I do not seek to spend too much time outside my cell. There are many rogues out there whose presence poses a genuine risk to life and limb. And why should I mix with all manner of criminals, I who have been put here because of a misunderstanding and the slanders of evil men? But what I find most difficult of all is living with the uncertainty I face here, as the weeks pass by one after another without any indication that the authorities intend to take any action against such a dangerous man. Sometimes when the chance arises I try to ask the watchmen or the Governor of the tower what will become of me, but receive little in the way of clear answers. Recently I asked yet again and could not help discerning some impatience on the part of the Governor, who seemed to suggest that I should think myself lucky as long as nothing was done in my case, because I could be sure of receiving a quick and final solution, an

67

Endlösung as he called it in German, running his index finger across his throat with a chilling laugh.

I feel that I am passing the time here in a dream or rather a nightmare, but I am not certain that I would wish to wake up from it to face a bleaker reality still. All my efforts are aimed at keeping my wits and not falling into despair.

Whether this is dream or reality, as I look back I obviously never imagined such a fate when I matriculated, with glowing hopes, from the school at Hólar. It is peculiar to reflect that it is only just over ten years since I set off in such fine spirits from Hólar, though admittedly with complete uncertainty ahead of me, and also a measure of apprehension in my heart about the evil eye that followed me from there, and the memory of the great adversity I had encountered.

At first, it looked as if my fortunes had permanently changed at last, and everything might have seemed to be going in my favour. It was no secret that I had completed my schooling with distinction and I felt I noticed how I had grown in stature in many people's eyes.

The climax to the turnaround in my fortunes, however, came when I had reached my resting place at Reynistadur at last, with my luggage. An incident had recently taken place there which at first sight seemed an utter tragedy, and could be described with the phrase in Ecclesiastes, that *all things come alike to all*. But it soon emerged that this occasion for sorrow, ample as it was, could also be regarded in a different light. What happened was that the clergyman at Reynistadur, a particularly fine young man of great integrity by the name of Thorgeir who had matriculated from the school several years earlier, had drowned while incautiously attempting to sit on his horse as it swam across the river Héradsvötn when he was somewhat the worse for drink. So a minister was needed in the parish, and with phenomenal speed Einar Arnfinnsson managed to win over everyone concerned, so that he was granted the benefice after the late Thorgeir, and was to be ordained at the earliest opportunity. Of course the office of deacon would also fall vacant at the same time.

It never entered my mind for an instant to seek that job. I did not dare to set my sights so high, despite my alleged excess of ambition.

Instead it was my friend Einar, ever trustworthy and loyal to me, who at once began talking to Monsignor Jón the King's Agent, who had nothing but good words for me from our acquaintance the previous summer and soon agreed to suggest to the Bishop at the first opportunity that I should be appointed as Einar's replacement in that post. Einar made every effort to prepare the ground wherever necessary before word spread too far and others who coveted the office could begin to make their move.

After playing this down at first, I soon saw that I was better suited to the post than most of the others I knew of, and it started to occupy my mind entirely. My opinion of myself grew, bolstering the rightful demands I felt able to make towards my future.

However, it was agreed that I should keep to my former plan of heading west for Bjarg to see my parents, but without committing myself so that I would be prepared to return to Skagafjördur if Einar sent me word; he expected to have the chance to clinch the matter when he rode over to Hólar to be ordained. So I was given the horse mentioned earlier and rode due west to the Húnavatn district. My first stop was Melstadur, where I met the Reverend Arngrímur who welcomed me warmly. He had heard of my matriculation and commented that I had played my cards right and used my talent wisely ever since he had tried to tug his copy of Donatus' *Grammar* back out of my hands by the hayfield wall those few years ago. We both laughed at this. When I told him the Bishop had offered to give me a reference, he said he could provide me with an even finer one, but that he would wait and see what the Bishop wrote in his letter, then double and redouble his words. Yet he said he suspected that a grant of money would come in more useful to me than any reference they could give, and he felt worst of all about the fact that, on account of his own slender means and his duty to educate his own sons, which would devolve upon his wife after his day, he had nothing to spare for my benefit, however much he would have liked to help me on my way.

I confided in him about the deaconry plan that was being hatched. He called it a wise move: it was a good idea to make a modest start, show and prove oneself. That noble man said he had no doubts that I would be a minister in a good benefice before very many years had passed.

I bade the Reverend Arngrímur a respectful farewell and he presented me with Calepinus' great dictionary of eleven languages, *Ambrosii Calepini Dictionarium unidecim linguarum*, as a parting gift. Afterwards I went on my way home to Bjarg and was welcomed by my parents. I had not been there for long, working like a Viking at all the jobs on the farm, when word came from Einar that the cat was in the bag, as he put it. I was greatly relieved.

I said goodbye to my parents at the end of the lambing season, telling them not to despair, though I had made only a short stay there and was leaving again, for now my fortunes had turned and I was on the path that must surely lead me to good office and advancement. I remember my father being nonchalant, while my mother said with some pride that she had always known this and I need not worry about them getting by.

Returning to Reynistadur, I could see how all the lobbying done by Einar and his fellow plotters had borne fruit and had the intended effect on the Bishop, who said he was eager to award me that office. I shall never really know how sincere his commitment was, but he could hardly avoid admitting that a man whom he had described as well qualified to study at the university must surely be capable of teaching children at Reynistadur and preaching sermons during the minister's absence if little were at stake.

Next I went straight from Reynistadur to Hólar to be examined once more and accept my office. The Bishop put me through an *examine theologicum* and could not find any fault with my knowledge. The following day I went to see him again in his quarters, where he was supposed to end by taking an oath from me and presenting me with the standard letter of commission as Deacon in nine articles, confirmed with the Bishop's seal.

It so happened that Thorleifur Kortsson the tailor was with him then, trying a half-sewn garment on him. He tacked the clothes, marked them here and there, pulled and tugged at the sleeves and eyed up the result with his single eye from various angles and directions, applying his measure to all His Holiness's extremities. This went on while the Bishop performed his official duties. I felt that the Bishop was slighting me with all this worldly fussing of his, and his attitude made my temper begin to rise. As a result, I perhaps guarded my tongue less than I should have, when the Bishop gave me his customary good wishes in my new office. I said I was happy about my advancement, so poor and common as I was. In itself that need not have been so bad, had I not chosen my words with such peculiar infelicity when, without thinking, I used a phrase I had heard copied from English fishermen. I accidentally said of myself and my own lack of means that I had definitely not been born with a silver spoon in my mouth.

The Bishop was speechless at first, then curtly told me to leave at once. Perhaps I had unwittingly made his ears prick up once more to all the slanders he would later be able to hear about me. And he did not have to look far to find one of the worst and most malicious slanderers of all, as would emerge later: Thorleifur Kortsson the tailor – who seemed to be one of the closest friends of the dispenser of my office – mincing around the Bishop on tiptoe with his needles and his pins.

Before leaving Hólar I managed to contact my dear Sigrídur from Stadarbakki and invited her there to hear a few words from me. I felt she was genuinely pleased at my advancement and told her I wanted to assure her that I had not forgotten her. We parted with warm words, and I was left pondering whether I had perhaps immersed myself too deeply in my books while I was at Hólar. Then I left that place yet again, on my way to my new office.

I almost warm right through, here in my cell full of rising damp, when I think back to the time of my deaconry. I increasingly realized what good fortune I had come into, since there could never be a finer opportunity for a matriculated student to devote himself to the pursuit of learning, if his inclinations lay in that direction, than in that office, besides the material benefits if he were industrious as well. I was given living quarters at the cloister and a maid by the name of Ásta was appointed to take care of my linen and my clothing, a very cheerful and sweet girl, desperately poor and rather playful in character, yet who served me with loyalty and great devotion.

In her own way, that girl was to play no small part in the course that my life was to follow, without anything occurring between her and me that might be considered of any consequence. However, I cannot avoid sometimes wondering whether my fortunes would have taken a different course had she been elsewhere at that time. Or would they? Misfortune would surely have found some other way to approach me.

Above all I call my days there almost an unbroken delight because at that time alone in my life, except for my stay at Melstadur and my best moments at school, I felt that I could see a bright future ahead and nurture the hope that everything would turn out in my favour, and that I was well on the way to reaping some rewards for my labours.

Yet I did not take life easy there nor live in the lap of luxury. I was expected to undertake all the duties that my superior, the King's Agent, demanded of me, and I did so without a word of complaint, including taking part in the haymaking, for which I was paid handsomely. Then

72

I went south with a team of horses to Reykjanes during that happy summer of mine as a deacon, to buy fish, and learned much from it about all that kind of business. I handled these and other tasks proficiently and with considerable satisfaction; after all, I have never scorned routine farmwork although my aspirations were towards learning.

Among the tasks I undertook was to go to Drangey island on the King's Agent's boat to catch birds, which was largely prompted by my yearning to see the place where Grettir the Strong lost his life; I felt a family obligation to do so, little as we resembled each other. I was also eager to see how hunters caught birds there on seaborne traps or by dangling from ropes over the cliff face, which I had had little chance to experience before.

A terrible vertigo came over me as I clambered my way up the rope on the cliff face after we arrived at the island, but I managed to reach the top in the end and was welcomed by the people who were already there. No one was allowed to go up there except their closest acquaintances. I was a stranger to them, but for the first time I felt the sweet power of status: the Deacon of Reynistadur was considered high-ranking enough to be a welcome visitor on Drangey island.

I roamed the length and the breadth of the island, studying the hunters' techniques and equipment, besides which I looked for relics at the place that I was reliably informed to be the ruins of Grettir's and Illugi's den, and I tried to put myself in the brothers' footsteps on the basis of the accounts in their saga. Hearing of my vertigo during the ascent, the islanders also told me an unfailing cure for fear of heights: to climb Drangey and then lie down, read the Lord's Prayer reverently and then fall asleep. Anyone who did so, they said, would be free of all such fears afterwards.

I followed their advice and it worked immediately, as I found out when I left the island by scaling down the same place as before without the slightest hint of fear. Conquering this fear has not proved particularly useful in my life, until now that I sit up in this sheer-walled tower, which could be called my private isle of exile.

Especially at night, when I observe the motions of the constellations by hanging out of my window, or sit up there reading my book.

While I was taking that short nap on the island I dreamed a dream that I could explain only a year later, when what was destined for my office had been fulfilled. I dreamed that Grettir the Strong himself appeared to me, warning me with a serious expression on his face never to forget how transient human fortune can be. I tried to joke with the old saga hero when I saw him frowning. I compared my spindly arms with his muscular ones and said I would surely be safe, assuming that the old saying from his saga was still true, that Fate and Fortune do not always go hand in hand. He fell silent at this and shook his head, frowning, strict and sad, and then I woke up.

Although I turned my hand to various things after arriving at the cloister, I felt that my official duties were the most worthwhile. I had my books and my quarters in the attic, and sat there engrossed in studies whenever I had the time, which was ample during the winter. There were also plenty of old books which had belonged to the cloister ever since the days of the papacy. Admittedly, most Catholic books had been destroyed, but many old treasures of Icelandic sagas and poetry had been preserved, and I became especially fond of those ancient tomes and all the lore that could be gleaned from them.

No less valuable was the companionship of my friend, the Reverend Einar. It was delightful to call on him in his quarters on one of the cloister's tied farmhouses; to join in his duties there, enjoy his cheerfulness and kindness like in the old days. And it was delightful, too, to discuss all manner of scholarship with him, for by that time he was already a learned man, very acute in all areas of theology and also the ancient lore of the North. He had made a particular study of legal writings and compiled a fine tract which he called the *Comb of Support*, about arrangements for the support of the poor and the aged in centuries past, with the aim of pointing out useful lessons for our own times to learn from. In places his writings tended to criticize various aspects of our legislation today.

When the chance presented itself I was allowed to preach in his place, and I could tell that my sermons were always well received and considered free from all heresy. I felt my resolve growing from one day to the next.

That autumn I started the teaching that was part of the Deacon's duties. A large number of boys were brought to Reynistadur at different times to be taught by me that winter. I found it easy to communicate with them and I think most of them left me somewhat wiser than when they had arrived. Some have since continued on the path of study, and perhaps benefited from some of the seeds that I may have sown among them.

But my relations with Einar were not confined to the spiritual. We were exuberant and enjoyed indulging in drink and tobacco. Sometimes we travelled around visiting various accomplished men whom we considered our friends, including Björn from Skardsá when he was not at Hólar. Our conversations ranged far and wide and we disputed matters great and small. Einar and I also regularly took sides in disputations, defending and attacking views as a rhetorical exercise, just as we had done at school. We bandied about a lot of entertaining ideas and perhaps some rather less intelligent ones, since we mainly did this simply for fun.

Our merry-making never went so far as to cause damage or earn us reproof, despite the claims to the contrary that would be heard later. The King's Agent never reproached us either, being somewhat fond of drink himself – sometimes embarrassingly so. He benefited from the fact that I continued to maintain my good contacts with merchants and foreign fishermen. I spent my pay on buying tobacco and spirits which I sold afterwards to interested parties at what I liked to call a reasonably extortionate price.

What always concerned me most about Einar was the lack of control he had over his lust for women. Despite urgings by his father and many worthy men, he never wanted to marry. He said he had no inclination to do so, since no woman deserved to be subjected to a lust such as his, he was too much of a gentleman for that. Instead he kept secret mistresses all around the district and the neighbouring farms, and often paid them visits at unusual times of day or met his female parishioners in improbable places to grant them even more improbable shrift or absolution. Many people knew about this, but none better than I, and I frequently warned him about it, but he always just laughed at me.

In fact, Einar took precautions; at least he seemed to manage somehow never to make any woman pregnant. Now that he had received his benefice it was more important than ever for him to avoid a pregnancy, which would have seen him defrocked and driven from his parish.

After Christmas that winter at Reynistadur I began to notice that Ásta, my maid, was involved with the Reverend Einar. She often paid him calls at night and some times she would sneak home late to attend to her duties. I disapproved, but let the matter rest. I have often thought since then that I should have been firmer on this point.

Should have, should not have, how trivial such words seem, now that everything has turned out the way it only could.

Everything seemed to be in my favour as my winter in the deaconry passed by. The pursuit of scholarship fuelled my poetic ambition and kindled my resolution to undertake something grander than mere epigrams and scurrilous verses. I began composing a ballad, taking my subject from Latin literature, a source I felt our poets had tended to neglect. The cloister had a copy of Ovid's *Metamorphoses*, which I read voraciously, and my fancy was soon caught by the story of Perseus, whom I chose to make the hero of my ballad. But because Ovid had told the story rather clumsily, omitting much that deserved to be included, I augmented it from Calepinus' *Dictionary* which the Reverend Arngrímur had given to me. I spent my spare time planning out the story and even began composing some verses as the winter drew on.

But the next spring, *anno domini* 1633, when everything seemed to be moving along smoothly, I suddenly received news one day that led my fortunes to take a sharp turn for the worse. What made my fall even greater was that I dared to think at first that the ominous tidings I heard might turn out to my advantage, as had happened to me before.

As with all fateful days, each moment appears to be firmly imprinted on my mind, although none of its trivial details seems to have played any part in those great tidings. Nor can I reproach my thoughts for failing to linger over those fragments while I sit on the windowsill of my prison, scarcely able to sift the chaff from the grain as my mind glides over that stage, inspecting the past as if it is in a mirror.

When I woke up in bed that morning, I could feel and hear that a beautiful day had already broken long before. It was a Monday. The day before, Einar and I had intended to discuss various matters after the church service, but had made the mistake of starting our meeting with a drop of spirit to loosen our tongues. Before we knew it, that single drop had become a whole deluge. We were soon drinking furiously, and went on for the rest of the day and well into the night. By then, attracted by the noise, the King's Agent and various other people had joined our company, until it turned into a public celebration. Einar and I drank far too much and smoked and chewed tobacco in excess, despite our earnest resolution to show moderation at all times. So less came of our wise discussions than we had intended.

Although I should have been on my feet long before, praising the Lord at the top of my voice for such a beautiful day, I awoke instead with a thundering headache, numb in all my limbs and joints, and feeling completely vacant inside. It would be true to say that I had no sense and no senses. Except for my body's urgent call for mercy, a bursting bladder which had woken me up in the first place and eventually sent me scrambling out from under my bedcovers, where I would have preferred to remain lying all day long. I sat down stiffly on the edge of the bed and reached out for the almost full chamberpot beneath it, but my hand was shaking so much that I immediately abandoned the idea of lifting it, knowing from experience that it was better to kneel.

Light poured in through the window from which the screen had been removed, I heard birds singing on the roof and lambs bleating farther off; the lambing season was at its height. I shook away the last drop, in great relief, then supported myself, my arms quivering, on the side of the bed, and tried to clear my throat. The outcome was an interminable cough that sent my ribcage moving up and down like the bag of a bellows, thrusting up the last dregs of winter and tobacco. I bent over to let the spit drop into the chamberpot, green on to yellow, blind to the world until Ásta suddenly came up to me in this wretched state and said, 'Oh, how fitting, the man of God is bowed in prayer. Of course it would not suit such a pillar of society to begin the day otherwise.'

And she flung my clothes on to the bed. I had not noticed her for my wheezing and coughing, until she had come right up to me, taunting me as usual, standing splay-footed above me, provocative and lithe, resting her hands on her slender waist, her hips thrust forth and her foot resting on the edge of the bed. Her supple calves greeted my eyes and I more than suspected the outline of her thighs beneath her skirt when I looked up askance at her and glimpsed her for a second from below, and I wondered whether she was trying to lead me astray.

But could Einar have had his way with her last night? I thought. Can you tell by looking at them? Surely they ought to have an ecstatic look about them, judging by Einar's descriptions of the pleasure he gave to all his lovers and his sweethearts. But that ecstasy could not have lasted long this time, I thought. On closer examination the girl gave a distinct impression of peevishness. However, the Minister was certainly no longer in the room where we had been drinking, when I came to my senses shortly before daybreak and crawled off back to my bed with great difficulty.

I hunched myself up to cover my nakedness from the girl's eyes, pushed the chamberpot under the bed and tugged a blanket over, wrapped myself in it and sat down with a sigh on the edge of the bed, and answered her – I remember every word – 'Oh, Ásta, that mouth of yours will get you into great trouble some day.'

But she was no more lost for words than ever, and snapped back, 'Says who? One of the biggest mouths that ever opened in north Iceland. No, I expect some other part of my body will get me into trouble before that happens. And some night rather than some day. Perhaps a different type of mouth too.'

Shocked to hear such language from a young lady, I reprimanded her in a fatherly tone, telling her that it was probably up to her what trouble she got into.

'Up it certainly is,' she said. Turned on her heel and was about to leave, then paused and looked back across her shoulder, saying in a low voice as if directing her words at the floor, 'If you should chance to meet the Reverend Einar later, will you tell him that I need to speak with him.'

On saying that she left and strutted away farther inside the house.

What now? I thought. Surely the clergyman didn't seek her out last night? Could he have found himself a new bedfellow? Yet again I wondered at Einar's firm resolution to live unmarried, even though by his own admission he could scarcely live a single night without a woman.

'They have their uses,' he would say of women, 'but it would be absurd to live with them.' That would mean hordes of children and constant disturbances, and he was too great a scholar to toss away his studies for such an uncertain prospect and doubtful gain.

Einar had behaved in this way ever since I first made his acquaintance in school. He had sweethearts all over the place. They were maidservants and farmworkers, women of high birth and housewives and beggarwomen. He also had many in sheepcotes on farms far and wide. And he was repeatedly visiting them by night and by day, whenever the chance arose, in beds and on benches, in passageways and in corners, beneath walls of stone and of turf, in hollows and on sloping banks, in the dark of the sitting room or out in the open, and even in the church attic. It all depended on the weather and the season of the year.

And Einar was incredibly bold in his habits, which certainly entailed some risk in these days when the provisions of the Great Edict were being followed through with their full force. Endless stories went around about couples who had succumbed to the temptation of various types of illicit love and paid a heavy price for it. It cost some their money, their reputation or even the skins from their bodies, while others were made to pay with their lives. But Einar never concealed his opinion that the edict was indefensible, a groundless law made by men with the sole purpose of confiscating people's money. He even cited the Bible itself to support his case; he needed only to point to Abraham's women and wives. Everyone dismissed this as sheer arrogance on his part, for they all knew what awaited him if anything were to go wrong, which they did not expect was very far off either.

But the fact remains that no matter what illicit acts may take place between a man and a woman, the authorities rarely seize on them unless a child is produced: the sin must be incarnated. Einar claimed to know diverse methods for preventing this. He said he could tell from women's eyes when there was a risk of conception, when he would either avoid them or discipline himself with the practice of Onan, as related in Genesis 38, verse 8, when Onan had to take his dead brother's wife and marry her: *that he spilled* [his seed] *on the ground, lest that he should give seed to his brother*. Einar dismissed as a lie the notion that Onan had indulged in humiliating self-abuse; rather, he had adopted the practice that Einar preferred to call *coitus interruptus*, and Einar said he could not understand why God disapproved of the method so strongly that he slew the resourceful Onan. Einar also claimed that old women had taught him other methods for preventing pregnancy, although for such crones the surest protection would have been offered by old age itself.

The light dazzled me once I had regained my strength enough to move about and stepped outside the front door. I lingered in the yard at first, to breathe in the exceptionally refreshing spring air. I saw Ásta come out through the door and huffily splash the contents of my chamberpot across the yard, then disappear back into the house.

Sensing another, gloomier mood beneath her cheerful exterior, I assumed Einar would know the reason. So I decided to take a stroll over the short distance to Holt where the Minister had his quarters. In particular, to find out whether he remembered any details about the night before that might still be hidden from me. I also intended to take the opportunity to borrow a few sheaves of paper from him, so that I could keep on with the ballad I was writing.

The Reverend Einar showed no more sign of suffering than ever. He had been up a long time, assuming of course that he had gone to bed at all. It was yet another trait of his that, if the occasion demanded it, he seemed to need far less sleep than other mortals. He was outside in the hayfield with his farmhands, busy with the ewes that were giving birth. His characteristic peals of laughter could be heard far away as he joked with the farmworkers. His peculiarly easy-going

81

temperament never changed. Somehow this was an integral part of the good fortune that had always shone upon Einar.

The Minister stood up beside a lamb as a ewe began to lick it fervidly. He leaned up against the farmyard wall when he saw me approaching and gave me a cheerful wave. 'Good day,' the Minister called, and I saw him produce his red kerchief from his sleeve, blow his nose loudly and brandish his snuff-box. Just as he had done when we first met almost five years before, by the rock on Hrísháls ridge as I walked in trepidation along Hjaltadalur valley, on my way to the school for the first time.

When I had walked all the way over to the wall where the Minister was standing, he handed me his snuff-box as he always did.

'Up and about? Have a pinch,' he said.

But I replied, 'Apparently I am. Anyway, I came to borrow some paper. I really must try to scribble something down today, after a night like that.'

'Yes, that was a sharp debate we had. And in the end you pretended you were overcome by sleep, when you'd run out of arguments.'

'If only I'd been in any state to pretend that! But Morpheus' spell left you untouched. You'd vanished without a trace when I woke up.'

The Reverend Einar looked away into the distance as he answered, 'Yes, oh yes. Duty always calls. I needed to visit a certain farm here. I shall say no more.'

We strolled off towards the house and went into Einar's study where I sat down in a chair while he opened his chest, counted out a few sheaves of paper and handed them to me.

'Is that enough? Just ask me if you need more. How's the ballad coming along? Won't you let me hear some of it soon?'

'It's just beginning to fall into place. I've mainly been collecting material, but toying with the odd verse as well, I'm just beginning to marry it up to the metre.'

Einar said he needed to tend to his lambs, so I made ready to leave, then turned around in the doorway, suddenly remembering the message I had been asked to deliver.

'Yes, while I remember, that poor creature Ásta asked me to tell you that she wants to see you when you have the time.'

Einar fell silent, then eventually sat down on his bed.

'Yes, I expect I can guess her errand,' he said.

'Is the passion beginning to wane?' I asked. 'Will she be leaving the camp? She's a lovely girl, although not of great family or overwhelming intellect. But why should she need to read anyway? Actually I had her in mind when I was trying to portray princess Danae in the first verse, let me see:

> Never was a nymph so fair
> made by nature men to snare;
> with panting breath her beauty's praise
> in poesy I must emblaze.

'Quite true,' Einar said. 'She's a lovely girl, however you look at her, a nymph so fair, and made by nature men to snare. Because it's happened, Gvendur, and steady yourself.' At which he looked up and looked straight at me. 'The fact is that your lovely maidservant is now expecting my child.'

dozed off from my thoughts up here in the window. I felt cold and hungry when I suddenly woke up to shouts, calling and footsteps coming from the palace grounds. I crawled closer to the window hole and cautiously stuck my head out between the bars, but dusk was falling and I could not see what was going on. Surely a troop of soldiers or guards coming or leaving. I turned my eyes towards the heavens. The dark fog that has lain across the city for some while had lifted. There was a new moon in the sky, shedding a pale light over the roofs and towers. At this sight I started to warm myself up by reciting a few verses from the love song in my *Second Ballad of Perseus*:

> Men grow hale and pour out ale
> from the horn which tributes keeps;
> in the second time of lunar prime
> the ancient fluid seeps.
>
> On heavenly tracks the moon doth wax,
> senses currents preening;
> it too decides the ebbs and tides,
> determines each dream's meaning.
>
> The lunar force maps out the course
> of memories and brains;
> each moon anew makes senses true
> then dims them when it wanes.

My slumber in the window was crazed with dreams, which mean nothing beneath such a moon, but one of the last things I remember was Einar telling me to hold on tight. Those were apposite words as I hung there and began to squeeze myself in again, bent stiff and fatigued.

Nor were they any less apt the first time Einar spoke them. My head reeled at the news and, having risen to my feet, I had to sink back into my chair. I felt it so outrageously out of place to hear such a thing, although this could be called merely the fulfilment of the inevitable, given Einar's character and carnal lusts. Now he would surely be defrocked, nothing else could await him, he would lose his ordination and office and be sentenced to pay a fine as well. And his eventual pardon would be at the Bishop's mercy; it was up to his superior to decide when and where but above all whether he would be readmitted to the clergy.

Be this as it may, it demonstrated once again that every man should look after himself. Despite my deep worries about Einar's welfare, I must admit that I had soon started pondering whether I would have to fear for my own position as a result. I was perfectly aware that I was in my office under Einar's aegis, and had been brought to Reynistadur through his influence. And I more than suspected that Bishop Thorlákur had not agreed to grant me that position and advancement with the happiest of hearts. Without a doubt, some people would have seen red at this arrangement. I felt I had performed my duties well and as far as I could tell the King's Agent who ran the cloister lands was well intentioned towards me, but would that be enough?

The Reverend Einar waited a while when he saw how taken aback I was by this news. He sat down and starting talking, and did not seem particularly anxious about his lot.

'It had to come to this,' he said. 'In fact I've been warned about it over and again. So I can probably safely start packing my bags soon. And I'm not exactly worried by it either. Not before the eyes of men, and even less God. I'll finish serving my punishment some time, then I can find myself a new office in another part of the country with other people, other women. What I feel worse about is if you have to suffer for it too and find your position here affected, Gvendur.'

But my thoughts had already gone well beyond that and were focusing on how I could turn all this to my advantage. I realized then that perhaps I might be able to capitalize on the outcome, so I answered Einar somewhat huffily, though I was staggered at the possibilities that I suddenly sensed ahead of me.

'Why should I suffer from it? Hasn't chastity been one of my greatest failings, in your opinion? Or have I got someone pregnant too? Is the Bishop supposed to think that I helped you, since my maid was involved? Perhaps that I lent her to you?'

'You know quite well, Gudmundur, how you came to be here,' Einar replied, 'and there's no love lost between you and the Bishop. He needs to plant his own people somewhere and plenty of them are eager to serve as deacons. All I meant was that when I'm no longer here to stand up for you, then maybe . . .'

But I interrupted him. 'Is any of them a better scholar than I am? And didn't the Bishop himself offer to write me a reference and urge me to go abroad to university? So why shouldn't he trust me as deacon up here on the edge of the world? I am asking too much if I want to hang on to what's really only a last resort?'

'All right, don't misunderstand me,' said Einar. 'Of course I know you deserve all this and more. But you ought to remember that perhaps the Bishop may have offered you a reference when he'd set his mind on getting rid of you from Iceland, because your presence always reminded him of that embarrassing episode with the silver spoons and the mockery and lampoons that followed it. And don't forget that sort of declaration didn't cost him anything, since you knew all along that you'd never be able to afford to go anywhere. Where's his reference then? Have you got it in writing?'

Though I may have known all this deep down, my anger welled up and I blurted right out what was preoccupying me and overshadowed everything else that Einar's troubles had already brought to light.

'My dear Einar,' I said, 'now that this misfortune has struck you I certainly don't intend to cower in fear of being swept up into it. On the contrary I plan to be bold and act by the old saying that one man's misfortune is another man's fortune. You tell me, if we forget all that old nonsense about kinship, family, blood and friendship and other trivialities, who ought to have a greater claim than I do to the office you are bound to lose now?'

'You know I haven't the slightest doubt that you're right,' he said. 'But I'm not the Bishop of Hólar.'

'And do you think it is fitting for the Bishop to make people pay for schoolboys' squabbles?'

'Maybe not, but it doesn't matter what is fitting if it doesn't fit.'

'Humble birth and poverty – are people supposed to accept that such things can hold them down for ever?'

'No, damn it, but there are plenty of other excuses to.'

Our conversation came to an end there and as time went by I became increasingly obsessed with that thought, and felt I could see more clearly than ever that I was about to make the best move of my life. And a shudder of joy ran through me when my thoughts went straight on from there to my dear Sigrídur from Stadarbakki. A man who was poised to become Vicar of Reynistadur would certainly have something to offer her. Since she had been so impressed with my deaconry, what about the status that was within my reach now? Now would be the time to ask for her hand. But would it be more fruitful to raise the question of marrying her before I sought the office, or apply for it first to strengthen my case when I proposed to her? Which course was more likely to support the other? In which order? Whatever happened, I would be wise to go over to Stadarbakki and have a good long talk with her mother, Gudrún, who had always taken me well despite what people said about her and her reputation for being devious if not downright brutal. She wouldn't care whether I already was a well-placed cleric or poised to become one. The crucial point was for her to hear what was in the offing and know that I was now a promising match and every mother's dream, before I launched on my marriage proposals. I swelled so much that I had to stand up and started pacing the floor inside the study.

My friend Einar must have sensed where my thoughts had carried me. He put his arm around my shoulders and gave me a friendly shake, as was often his custom.

'Don't get excited, you know where it can lead you. No, no, of course not. Try it, by all means. But I should warn you against over-optimism. I'll support you in your resolution, mainly behind the scenes perhaps, because you can hardly call me much of a champion of good causes after all this. But you ought to have plenty of time to set everything up. No one knows what's in the offing yet apart from the two of us and Ásta, and it will still be a long time before she starts showing. If you use your time well and prepare the way for yourself by leading an exemplary life here, cut back on drink and tobacco, nothing in excess, then I'm certain everyone will have nothing but kind words to say about you. I can make sure that you take every sermon you can and build up your eloquence, spirit of mind and fervour of prayer. And if you devote yourself to your studies and keep in good contact with Björn from Skardsá, there'll be some good words in the Bishop's ears from that quarter. Yes, you never know . . .'

'It also occurred to me,' I added, 'whether I shouldn't go over to Melstadur to see Arngrímur and have him put in a word for me too. I have to go to Midfjördur any way.'

'I'll see to that. Don't you go roaming all over the place for the time being. I expect to go to the West myself before autumn, so that at least my parents find out what's going on at first hand. I could drop in on our wise old friend then. It's true, his word carries a lot of weight, because the Bishop can never ignore the fact that he snatched away an office he never deserved from right under Arngrímur's nose. If everything falls into place there might be a chance that the plan will work out. But you watch yourself. Don't be overzealous and try to think before you act. You know what the Bishop always criticized you for – your temper and your mouth.'

'Most of that was lies and slanders.'

'Plus the odd lampoon if I recall correctly.'

'They never come unprovoked. But I did let fly a few when I was unfairly attacked.'

'Rather too quickly. You must learn to control yourself.'

That summer passed, turning out cold and wet in north Iceland, and the land and sea failed to provide, with scant and poor hay and meagre fishing. Winter fell early with swirling snowstorms and frosts, felling people and animals in droves throughout the countryside.

Near the end of November Ásta gave birth to her child at Reynistadur after a difficult labour. It was a boy who was slow to gain strength and did not live for long. As expected, Einar readily and willingly acknowledged the child as his own, never having tried to conceal from anyone that he was responsible for her pregnancy. So everyone knew the child's paternity long before it was born.

Early that autumn, the Reverend Einar went on his own initiative to see the Bishop, explained what had happened and what would happen, and said he would take the consequences and knew they could not be avoided. He was reproached and admonished heavily, then immediately stripped of his ordination and removed from his clergyman's office, and told to leave by no later than the end of the year. The following spring he and Ásta were both sentenced for having a child in fornication, their first offence each, in accordance with the strictures of the Great Edict, and I heard that Einar paid the fine for them both. Ásta soon left Reynistadur, intending to go to her family farther up north. I was sad when I said goodbye to her and I have neither seen nor heard of her since.

Einar himself moved away just after Christmas. At first he stayed with his parents at Stadur, then went travelling soon after and stayed at many places over the next few years. He worked as a farmhand in different parts of the country during the summers, and was a teacher here and there in the winters. He also worked on boats during the fishing season and earned a good reputation everywhere he went, since he was a very strong man and energetic at any job he undertook.

While Einar was awaiting his fate, I had tried to prepare for my prospective ordination into the clergy in various ways: I read furiously and tried as best I could to live a pure life. I also began preparing to make my betrothal. Both because I considered this necessary in the end for any man who does not wish to wither away in sinful contemplations, and also because I suspected that the Bishop preferred his clergymen to be married, not least after Einar's matter had arisen.

As I had planned, I wrote a long letter to the parents at Stadarbakki, Gudrún Jónsdóttir and her husband Gissur Gamlason, seeking the hand of her honourable maiden daughter, Sigrídur Jónsdóttir, presently residing at Hólar. I gave myself plenty of time to compose the letter and repeatedly went over the wording to ensure that it showed me in the best of lights, but without giving too strong an impression of arrogance. I mentioned that I was already the incumbent of a spiritual office and described my present humble post as a clear pointer towards something different and greater. I strongly suggested what was in the offing, but without stating anything outright before I had clinched it. I considered my approach outstandingly shrewd and was certain that it would seem irresistible. I also mentioned my strong yearning to apply for a position, in the course of time, near to my home district. This was an other subtle ploy (I thought) since I knew they were determined to see Sigrídur married to a clergyman who could be expected to take over the vicarage at Stadarbakki, where the couple could have one corner to themselves in their old age.

Before autumn I asked Einar to take the letter with him on his way to Hrútafjördur. When he returned he said he had told the Reverend Arngrímur about my proposal, and in the meantime that fine old man had gone to see his sister and put in a very good word for me. Einar, too, said he had never spared my praises and that for all he could see, my marriage prospects looked splendid.

Sensing a good wind in my sails no matter where I turned, I began to soar in spirit, so overboldened that I felt I had the whole world in my hands. In this frame of mind I decided to act and went over to Hólar not long after Einar had left. I marched straight in to see the Bishop and was certainly very self-confident and upright, almost perpendicular, as I stated my errand without beating about the bush and without any humility either. I said I wanted to become Vicar of Reynistadur now that the Reverend Einar was no longer serving there.

Bishop Thorlákur took a long look at me, then said curtly, shaking his head, that the idea was absolutely absurd and I could not be in my right mind to allow myself to think of such a thing. I was far too lowly for such preference, and at the same time sharp-tongued and quick-tempered, a malicious lampooner and a provocateur. There was no more to be said about the matter, since many other people, some of them experienced and respected clerics, were also seeking a good office like Reynistadur. Surely I had to admit, he said, that it had not worked out to send such a young and dandyish man as Einar there, even though he was from a clerical family.

I tried not to be upset by his words and replied at once that however it turned out, whichever Vicar went there, some other office would thereby fall vacant and I would like to be granted that instead.

Instead of answering, the Bishop looked at me with a peculiar expression on his face, even a hint a fear, and looked towards the door as if checking the escape route. He said that I should go back home. I would be called in if I was ever needed to serve in the clergy. He could consider the matter again if the office on Grímsey island fell vacant, which would hardly be in the next few years unless something very unexpected happened. But I should beware of treating his words as the equivalent of a promise.

Thereby my audience came to an end, in what I felt was total uncertainty, and I was badly dissatisfied with my lot. Little did I know that my lot was already even worse than I could ever have suspected.

After I had been rebuffed from the Bishop's table, I had reached the door when he called out to me, 'Did you never learn, Gudmundur, the noble words that Socrates and many men after him adopted as their own true commandment? Namely: *know yourself.*'

I said I had, but the Bishop said, on the contrary, if that were right I would hardly have allowed myself the liberty of aiming so high. His last words to me were these, 'Gudmundur, learn to *know yourself.*'

At this I went home and saw my journey as an absolute failure. But though this was hard to live with immediately afterwards, having had much grander plans for myself, I was eventually persuaded by my good friends into consoling myself with what I had anyway. I still had my deaconry, after all, and could continue developing and enriching myself and my spirit. And the response to my overtures of marriage would surely still be in effect and be ready to bloom when my fortunes began to improve again.

I had not been immersed in these thoughts for long, consoling myself and building myself up again, when the next shock came, followed by what could be called the blow that would put me out of my misery. When the new Vicar appeared there in the spring we were all dumbfounded. The great cleric and paragon who was to take Einar's place was none other than dim-witted Magnús, who once urinated on my mattress at Hólar, nephew of Sheriff Gudmundur and partly brought up at his house in Thingeyrar.

I was definitely shaken when I saw the new Vicar, but calmed down when I began to wonder whether his advancement might turn out to be my gain in the long run. Knowing me to be far superior to him in all learning, preaching and qualities of the mind, the parishioners would soon realize what a terrible choice had been made. And since poor old Magnús was inexperienced and ill-qualified for anything other than urinating on mattresses, I saw that I could make him dependent on me by assisting him as best I could, then eventually manipulate the situation so that he was incapable of doing anything without my support. I would be the true Vicar of Reynistadur, thereby trumping the trick played by the court at Hólar. In the end, it would be perfectly clear who was what.

With these thoughts in my mind I greeted Magnús with an affection and sycophancy that I can hardly recall without blushing, welcomed him and called him my friend and brother, but his only reaction was to spit, so to speak, on my outstretched hand of reconciliation. He asked huffily what I was doing still hanging around there. And when I mentioned my office and said I was there in that capacity, he said he had never heard the like and asked whether I pretended not to know that the Bishop had expelled me from the deaconry for more than ample grounds.

Naturally taken aback, I went at once to ask the Agent to tell me the whole story, but he was nowhere to be found; the ground seemed to have opened up and swallowed him. Magnús said there was no need for the Agent to confirm anything, since he brought everything with him in writing. Then he produced some papers from his bags and showed me a letter which said, without naming any charges and with no word of explanation, that I had been expelled from my office.

I was close to fainting when I read it, but soon recovered my senses and rode off to Hólar at once to demand a further explanation from the Bishop, but was not granted an audience. I tried to have the Bishop informed that I was ready to answer to any charges that had been made against me, but the only reply I received was silence.

Then I tried to have a word with Sigrídur before leaving, for our friendship and old time's sake, but was simply told that she was not there. I was surprised, but did not understand until later.

I was in a gloomy mood when I returned to Reynistadur after this fruitless journey. Without speaking a word to anyone, I gathered up my humble belongings and old books in my trunk and some sacks, and left them in a shed while I went over to Skardsá where I could always be sure of borrowing a horse to ride to Bjarg. I caught a glimpse of the King's Agent at the cloister while I was walking away, but he quickly vanished behind a wall, kept out of my way after that and pretended to be mending the buildings. Clearly he was not overcome by desire to meet me, since he had probably given me less support than I had expected from him.

My friend Björn welcomed me to Skardsá and invited me to stay there for a few days while I licked my wounds. He had just returned from Hólar, where he had spent some time writing. After making a lot of inquiries there he could tell me plenty of the background to my dashed hopes. He would not blame the Agent at the cloister for anything, and thought he had spoken up for me as best he could, only to be countered with accusations of drunkenness and debauchery and filth with Einar and myself, and outrageous distortions and exaggerations about our merrymaking, lively though it certainly was at times.

It was clear from what Björn said that the Bishop had acted on the basis of gross slanders about me, and instead of investigating the truth of the accusations he had readily believed all those evil tales about me, which was doubtless the price I had to pay for the earlier friction between us.

It was the family from Thingeyrar who were behind this evil slander: Sheriff Gudmundur Hákonarson and his nephew, the Bishop's special tailor Thorleifur Kortsson, who snuffled like a dog around him and the entire court at Hólar as he fitted them with the clothes he cut. Björn thought that Gudmundur had played out his nephew Magnús deliberately to block my advancement, clearly starting to believe that I would soon actually be offered the ministry at Reynistadur.

In the uncle's and nephew's opinion there was precious little of which I was not guilty, and most of the adversity that they and their family had encountered for years on end seemed to be attributable to me. My insinuations to little Páll Björnsson rebounded badly on me, too, since for all his great intelligence he had still not grown out of his fear of sorcery. He and Thorleifur had become close friends while they were at Hólar together after I left, and were always working each other into a frenzy about the black arts. Páll chipped in stories of the manifold brutality and pranks performed by Icelandic sorcerers, while Thorleifur replied by describing the latest developments abroad in combating these fearful human beasts and the progress being made in designing tools and equipment to enable the authorities to exact confessions increasingly easily.

Because of his sloth and incapacity for learning, Thorkell Gudmundsson had abandoned his studies and left the school. His relatives were now claiming that I had been the main cause. Thorleifur backed up this claim with countless examples of the way I had deluded Thorkell with my magic spells and brought misfortune on his school career with my poetry and curses. It was convenient for Sheriff Gudmundur to believe every word, since he was known to be over-burdened with anxiety at the ineptitude his only son showed for learning, despite being given every possible chance.

I learned all this and much more during those days with Björn at Skardsá. Then he lent me a horse and I went straight back to Reyni-stadur. There I met the Agent of the cloister, Monsignor Jón, who was quite drunk; we talked the matter over and he convinced me for once and for all that he had played no part in bringing about my demise, but confirmed Björn's story as far as it concerned him. Monsignor Jón also told me that the Bishop had ordered him to inform me of my dismissal and make sure that I left. Because of our good friendship, he said, he had not felt up to doing this, but had hidden in the outhouses instead and had been drinking heavily.

A new Deacon was expected in my place. The Bishop had decided to appoint one of his relatives, a certain Eiríkur, nicknamed 'the Coward', who had matriculated a few years before me and had never settled down anywhere since, because he could never make decisions. He was the nephew of Skúli from Eiríksstadir, who was the father of Bishop Thorlákur. That was his one merit.

Monsignor Jón was very downcast about how everything had turned out, but felt it was obvious that he could do nothing. He compared it to the lame leading the blind, having those two intellectual midgets preaching the Holy Scriptures. It was a great turn for the worse to have them instead of Einar and myself, such learned and inspired men. Those were his very words.

In the end we drank a farewell toast together, after he had paid me the wages that he owed me for my services. Then I tied my bags on to the horse I had borrowed from Skardsá, mounted it and cantered off from Reynistadur for the last time. I headed for the West, for Midfjördur, yet again in swirling, drifting snow, and more often than once I was convinced I would freeze to death. My vision grew darker and darker as I approached my childhood haunts.

And there I was back at Bjarg for good, with no other prospect than the end of my scholarly career and all hopes of advancement in the spiritual field. For all that, I would not admit yet that I had been beaten down completely. I considered that given the response my marriage prospects had met at Stadarbakki, and Sigrídur's positive feelings towards me, I had no reason to expect anything but acceptance of my proposal, in spite of everything. I imagined our future as a worthy farming family back at Bjarg, and was obstinate enough to suppose that this would be enough to win her hand. With this in mind I went over to Stadarbakki, intending to discuss with Madam Gudrún how determined I still was, despite this change in my plans.

But when I arrived the old woman wouldn't even listen to me. On the contrary, I was driven right away with curses and horrendous insults and threats of violence or death if I so much as showed my face around there again. Fierce dogs were set on me and I barely escaped from them, my heels bitten, panting for breath, with no shoes on and my trouser legs hanging in tatters.

In this state I turned up at Melstadur where I learned from the Reverend Arngrímur that a party had been sent from Hólar to Stadarbakki specifically to slander me by warning his sister Gudrún of the great danger that I posed. Thorleifur Kortsson had been one of the ringleaders on this errand, and was welcomed there. Gudrún had then assigned him the task of standing guard over Mistress Sigrídur at Hólar, to prevent me from speaking to her. Arngrímur said that he had tried to complain to his sister but met no response at all, and said there was no hope that she would ever change her mind on the matter.

Arngrímur gave me some physical nourishment but my spirit remained unresponsive, and after taking a rest I crept off home as if abandoned by fortune, and my depression descended on me as never before. I was quite familiar with such moods and knew that they always followed great passions which had kindled excitement within me. But this went further than ever before; I broke down and turned languid and was confined to bed, scarcely speaking a word other than delirious nonsense for almost half a year. I hardly remember it myself, but was told about it when I came back to my senses. My mind became so benighted that I felt I would never reclaim my happiness, and thus the winter passed, right through to the summer in absolute madness.

I did not begin recovering until after Midsummer Day, when my mother finally managed to persuade me to get out of my bed and go into the yard in brilliant weather to behold the glory of creation. In the end I gave in to her persuasion and crawled out. As I leaned up against the wall on my wobbly legs to prevent myself from falling over, and squinted into the brightness, my mother made a pronouncement that woke me from my sickly coma.

She said that I was in a terrible state and had been completely unrecognizable ever since those evil people from Skagafjördur had tricked me. Her words suddenly prompted me to recall what the Bishop had said to me in parting: '*Know yourself*, learn to *know yourself.*' And at this memory I started to reflect on which of the two of us knew himself better, I who had now dived down to the depths in my madness, or the Bishop in the self-contentment of his own authority. When I lay down again some time later, thoughts began to pour in upon me from all directions and I resolved to feed them all into a meaty satire about it.

The following morning I woke up in normal health, almost in light spirits, and got out of my bed, ate heartily and put on some new clothes that my mother had ready for me in my trunk. Afterwards I took out a few sheets of paper, stirred my ink well and chose a pen. Then I went outside in the beautiful summer weather and settled myself down beside the hayfield wall, resting my sheets of paper on a plank, and started writing. Before I knew it I was writing furiously, swamping the Bishop and his lapdogs with my scorn.

It soothed my wounded mind to find words for my thoughts about the humiliation that was wrought upon me. I wrote it out of me, and me out of it. Likewise my suffering here in this prison is soothed and eased while I lie here on my mattress, close my eyes and try to bring back almost word for word that piece of writing which once unburdened me of my misery.

ΓΝΩΘΙ ΣΕΑΥΤΟΝ, *nosce te ipsam*, *know yourself* or *learn to know yourself*, these were the words the wise old pagans considered no human being could be without, and saw this art as originating more from celestial wisdom than earthly wiles or the many-sensed reasoning of human nature.

But that which is admired is not easy to guard, and a worthwhile good often costs a pretty price. So to *know yourself* is easier said than done. Asked what was the most difficult thing for a man to do, someone once answered, 'To know yourself without pretending to.' Then he was asked what was easiest of all. 'To pretend to know other people,' he said.

Certainly it is celestial wisdom to know yourself and guide men through the narrow and treacherous street which leadeth to life. But what sort of wisdom can it be not to pay heed to oneself in any way or to consider oneself an unpunishable angel, and scout and search instead to count the flaws and qualities of others, or be able to find fault with everything about them but nothing at all with oneself? More people would do better to pay heed to that. Pity others in much, but yourself in little. Our Lord refers to this in his image of the mote and the beam in the eye.

But that wide road is so repeatedly trodden that it is easy to follow. It is simplest of all things to accuse others, charge them with some thing and misinterpret their intentions as evil. This is a common ploy and used unsparingly. But it is a difficult task to follow a narrow path, to approach yourself and see mainly flaws, especially when you are doing well and fortune flatters you.

This is not to claim that I myself have mastered the precious and most fortuitous art to know myself or can teach it to others by. None the less, I have had the privilege of learning a method towards this, and it would be remarkable if I had no knowledge of my own weaknesses. I have been so crushed in the mortar of the most dangerous temptations, then ground up by the gnashing teeth and molars of mendacious backbiters and spreaders of slander, besides my companions from birth, namely poverty and lack of property and helpers.

To speak right out, I call them liars who say that I pretend to be much better than I am. Because by my own example I have constantly been aware and demonstrated that I am one of the weakest and most helpless of all beings, and most guilty of sin before God, if He cared to pass judgment upon me. God Himself has taught me that directly and indirectly with the testimony of conscience. But by God's mercy I am still what I am, and His gifts to me are not so humble that they might not be used to some good purpose, if I knew how to apply them and they were not thwarted by jealousy. Those who want to accuse me of the opposite should surely pay heed to whether I myself revel in my helplessness and humiliation. 'For God has often been the greatest towards the smallest,' said St Bernard of Clairvaux, 'or lent wits and sense to those who lacked riches.'

Here I shall set down a parable to show that men of great standing and those who are rich in pride are more prone to pretend to be good and worthy than poor people who are wearied by adversity, who cannot rise for the melting heat from richer men's golden suns.

A calf, while it is young and of little weight, is harmless to any child. It is drawn to those who feed it, since the calf knows where his pail and manger are. But when it has become an old ox or bull, it is dangerous to men, assertive and irritable, violent and aggressive; it butts and stamps, bellows and screeches as if invincible. Yet nothing more awaits it than the blow from a sledgehammer or a murderous knife. Is there not a moral implied here, that poverty and humble origins hinder many people from doing anything excessively ambitious, so that the same person has a good conscience as a result? But of the others it can be said that a man should be heeded when he may do as he pleases.

Another parable. While a woodland shrub is young and little grown, any lamb can reach its leaves and consume them. But when the oak is fully grown, the nimblest of woodland animals cannot reach its branches, so high does it stretch itself out, and the birds of the air rest there unthreatened. And any man who wants to reach and pluck its fruits must have a ladder for the purpose.

The same applies to unimposing laymen and men of lowly birth. From them any man can avail himself of the good will and consideration that can be obtained from them. They bestow this with no excess of effort, while lofty men of noble birth – it is not within everyone's reach to acquire the favours that they are entrusted with bestowing, especially promotion and the offices of more noble classes, which are attainable only by seeking them at their lordships' very pinnacle.

But a man who strives to reach there may have a ladder ready, prop it up against that unassailable oak and scale it. The struts of that ladder shall be the Christian religion, pure and unpolluted, and the ethics of men of true faith.

The first rung should be *prayer* and devotion to the service of God in evangelical office.

The second, *virtue* and fear of God, with God-fearing and irreproachable action.

The third rung ought to be *art*, education and study in the written arts and the scholarship of the teachings.

The fourth, *spirit of mind*, likewise to present these qualities rationally for the necessary service of those who are so ordered. I expect that health and wholesomeness of life and limbs should be included, so that they are neither one-handed nor one-eyed.

With this ladder many succeed well in acquiring from the lap of privilege ample respect, and be this well, and may they enjoy it.

Again, those others are no fewer who never come close to this ladder and move farther from its rungs. They have extra rungs fitted clumsily into it, yet still scale it and proceed in the same way:

In that case the first rung is *bribery* and *intermediacy*, for it is stated so: *non prece sed precio*, office is not acquired by prayer, but

101

by mortgage of land and a handful of ornate things on which the names of kings are inscribed, or precious articles that are loaded into chests.

Instead of virtue, some help themselves with the *following* and *persuasion* of supporters, relatives, parents or guardians, and that suffices them.

Thirdly, in place of learning and education, some profit by being *the kin of the curds but married to the milk*, or by entering into marriage, even though it is only the affiliation of a distant relative, while those who are closely related allow that to suffice.

In the fourth place, instead of intelligence, many are served by the *worldly spirit* of benefactors and influential friends. If the closest friend of the provider of office is in that company, it helps next to God (if not more than God), and the same person does not seem to want for any gift, though he may have behaved with the habit of a dog or is as one-eyed as Odin in times of old.

Not to know yourself, this is the more befouling the higher it takes place, for although the shoes pinch or the legs are muddy, this may be well tolerated. But closer to the forehead, if the brows are besmirched, this spells doom to the eyes and tribulation to the heart.

So it is also with those who have nothing to do and can apply themselves to little, have no rank to administer. Though stupidity blinds them and clouds their eyes so that they do not know themselves, that may be suffered to go its own course.

But if superiority places such a high value on itself and says: I do nothing but God's will, He governs me and my biddings entirely. *Item*, they claim to make obedience to God when they banish men beyond their authority for the sake of empty lies, shake them off with violence and wrath and say they are doing right. This is a devilish way to know yourself, paying little heed to the good counsel: *quanto es sublimior, tanto te geras submissius*. That is: Be the more submissive, the higher you sit, because the higher placed falls the lower. *Qui sedet inferius non habet unde cadat* – you can't fall off the floor.

But just as it is necessary for a man to know himself, it is no less useful for him to know good from evil, or distinguish evil from good. But perhaps most of us die without learning this properly in many things.

The first error of man in Paradise was to steal from the tree of knowledge. *Item*, man did not know lies from the truth. The same error has prevailed ever since and will be the last for the children of the world, both in learning and living, for Satan gilds much that is dark underneath and does so in his own way on each occasion, but the trick is the same, to pollute the truth with lies and make a changeling from a legitimate child, that is hypocrisy from holiness. Of the error of learning and on the subject of religion I have nothing to say in this country's sphere. God has made His consecrated word glow so much here with the beautiful evening sun that no shadow has fallen for a long time and the Devil's fog has had to yield, whether he has wanted to or not he has allowed that to be. But so that he, that evil and wary visitor, does not sit here idle although the dice do not fall as he bids, he plays what turns up until a new round may commence. Since he cannot hinder the lesson of God's word, he sits in ambush to hinder the happiness of God's children and corrupts the actions and behaviour of society's ranks. Because he cannot lead religion astray, he strives to bring illness upon administration, so that it shall not be well performed, doing this so as to make the most people deserve double punishment, in that they know their Father's will but do it not. Then Earl Satan snaps his fingers at having brought this to pass, saying that he will not protest if God's word is taught uncorrupted and pure, as long as no one or few abide by it.

But to inveigle himself he blinds the prying lady of mankind, our hidden lady, I mean carnal wisdom, so that man does not know good from evil or has no conscience about it, dressing the wolf in lamb's clothing. That is, makes vice and crime seem the acts of angels. Ye shall be as gods, he said to Eve, if you take that which is forbidden, that is your fortune. Likewise many people still today polish the injustice which they and their friends perform at the urging of the betrayer, and it comes to pass as Ecclesiastes says: *there be just men, unto whom it happeneth according to the work of the wicked; again, there be wicked men, to whom it happeneth according to the work of the righteous.*

What is the reason? Yes, people do not know lies from virtue, deceit from modesty, discretion from injustice. Many things are done in the name of goodness that are nothing but wrongfulness. Saul had David condemned as a traitor, thinking he was acting well and rightly. Ahab had Michaiah confined to a prison, because they thought they had God's approval upon them.

But examples do not need to be sought from ages past or other countries – in Iceland has the Devil not poured mendacious slanders on to a weak, innocent, wretched man, using as his agents men who are overbold of deed and word, then let a second and a third strike the wound again with the murderous weapon of an evil tongue? And his master has managed the situation so badly that, instead of defending his rearguard and championing truth and innocence, he has applied the unction so as to accuse the very one who was in the right, and deprived him of his office and order, without trial, without law, without summons, without interrogation, lending both his ears to lies and neither to the truth, and considers himself to have acted justly on God's behalf, though men may say: Everyone deserves a hearing.

Item: As the Governor Festus said to the Jews about Saint Paul: It is not the custom of us Romans, he said, to sentence anyone until he has accusers in a court, thereby giving him the chance to defend himself. *Nam si accusasse sat est, quis innocens erit?* If nothing need be done but to accuse, few would be pronounced innocent; the small may be writ large.

If the most keen-eyed of men, who ought to be the vanguard of the congregation, are so blinded by darkness, what then of us mules and toilers who can hardly look up for fighting our struggle against poverty? They think they are doing good, and reap the benefits if they do good. Their share will be measured for them or their offspring in the same measure. But God forgive them, they know not what they do. I assume it is caused by their not knowing right from wrong, or else they shall be judged without their prayers being heard.

What it all boils down to is, I would give my thanks for the congregation if someone knew himself.

At first I had no other intention than to keep my writings to myself and take them out for my own diversion. I felt that it had been a worthwhile exercise in its way, acting as a genuine cure and relieving me of the great illness of mind that had come close to finishing me off completely. I was capable now of dealing with people and working again, and had begun to set my sights forward, though I hardly had the faintest idea where that path might lie. It is not the smallest of fortunes to forget that which cannot be retracted, or, as Ecclesiastes says somewhere, if I recall correctly: *It is better to tend well to that which is in the hand than to regret that which is foregone and will never be reclaimed.*

As time went by I began to hear from various quarters that the Bishop and the men in his charge often said that it was just as well that they had succeeded in driving me out of my deaconry in good time and hindered my further advancement before I wrought more damage, now that it had come to light that I was absolutely mad and rarely in my right mind.

When I became aware of this I began to show my writings without compunction to some of my friends who said they liked them, laughed out loud and sometimes copied them out. Eventually I had cunningly arranged everything in my writings to leave myself free of all exculpation, yet in such a way that the targets of my barbs would surely understand them. Very soon I heard that my work had spread widely and was being passed around in copies. I did not mind giving as many people as possible the chance to judge whether this man was totally crazed, who could scathe his accusers and enviers so humiliatingly and cleverly.

I did not fear in the slightest when my little work went into circulation and did not pay heed to whether it might reach the Bishop and chill his feelings towards me even more. I knew I had arranged my words in such a way that he would have had trouble in finding grounds for attacking me without having to admit at the same time to many of the reproaches that were delivered upon their unnamed lordships. By then I felt we had settled our differences for once and for all, and the Bishop could hardly become more opposed to me than he already was anyway.

About Gudrún at Stadarbakki I wrote a long satire which spread far and wide and people laughed at it and danced to it in Midfjördur. In this way I took a late vengeance, futile as it was, which comforted my mind for a while.

The poem included these verses about Thorleifur Kortsson and other of the bishop's men, and their dealings with the old woman:

> Stir up your slanders and wiles,
> your backbiting, nonsense and biles,
> whose words and malicious guiles
> have chilled me and unmanned
>   – here is my hand.
> Send your tongue a-gallop for miles,
> I trust you to speak in this wise,
> you have found it easy awhiles
>   to tell at Bakki, to tell at Bakki your lies.

> One man I could trust for sure,
> he spoke with a hero's braveur
> then opened his silver-tongued store
> and his papers as planned
>   – here is my hand.
> His slander at last out he bore
> and shook his little mane,
> trussed his bales of deceit the more,
>   whispered at Bakki, whispered at Bakki again.

Eighteen trusses of lies he unpacked,
those words did her wonder attract,
at such food her lips she smacked,
to store with her hate's contraband
    – here is my hand.
Due praises, my lord, you have lacked,
from my heart I thank you for all.
Like a mother to you I shall act
    as long as at Bakki, as long as at Bakki I rule.

Here you shall dress and dine,
be shod with vellum fine,
drink France's noblest wine
and wear clothes full grand
    – here is my hand.
They drank for their souls to entwine
and gloated over their plot,
he was metamorphosed to a swine,
    his heart at Bakki, his heart at Bakki grew hot.

Down to the cellar he passed,
his thirst was mighty and vast,
from his cups up he rose at last
drunk as a pig, to stand
    – here is my hand.
Kisses flew hard and fast,
like lapdogs licking away,
cheered by their minds' evil cast,
    it is good at Bakki, it is good at Bakki to stay.

Pigs love filthy heaps and swill,
ravens pluck out eyes and kill,
in darkness ghosts do as they will.
My words you will understand
    – here is my hand.

> Lapdogs care not their thanks to spill
> for silver or gold, not a jot;
> anyone with a belly to fill
>   off to Bakki can trot, off to Stadarbakki can trot.

I now devoted myself entirely to the chores on my parents' farm at Bjarg. They were delighted and did not seem to regret my spiritual career meeting such a sorry end. They thought it worth much more to have retrieved me from the paralysing claws of madness. By that time they were growing weary, especially my father who was well advanced in years and little able to work on account of his stiffness and all kinds of ailments.

Several years passed and I was reasonably contented with my lot, under the circumstances. Admittedly, the rough came with the smooth and although my spirits tended to plummet from time to time I managed to avoid the ultimate abyss, and conversely I could soar like an eagle when I was in the right mood and the fancy took me. I energetically undertook all the tasks on the farm, but most enjoyed going off for provisions of various kinds, such as on fishing trips to Snaefellsnes or to buy stockfish in south Iceland.

My farming kept us well and I made a certain amount of money, and resumed my old practice of acquiring tobacco and spirits and keeping them in stock, to sell to my neighbours and others at a handsome profit. I also served these goods liberally to my guests, my friends and not least myself. When my father eventually died from his illness after much suffering in spring 1646, an exceptionally inclement season which caused widespread deaths, I became the breadwinner on my mother's farm.

Although for the time being I had put aside all notions of advancement in office or going abroad to the university, and was preoccupied with the crofter's routine toil, I never abandoned my devotion to scholarship and remained as best I could in contact with all the fine friends I had made in that field, such as Björn from Skardsá, the Reverend Arngrímur and many other wise men. Occasionally in the winters I would call on farms in the North to teach young people there, and I prepared many lads for going to school. I was well spoken of by many of the better-off farmers who approached me for such help.

I also made an effort to continue the serious pursuit of poetry that I had embarked on while I was at Reynistadur. I resumed my *Ballads of Perseus* and finished them, in six parts. I included some love songs drawn from the tribulations I had suffered and fired off a good few broadsides which were aimed, implicitly and explicitly, at unjust men of authority. Then I returned to the treasure-house of classical lore and garnered material from it for my *Ballads of Bellerofonti*, reworking it in a much more elaborate style and taking much longer over it, but succeeded in the end. I wrote many more things at this time, such as my *Metrical Key* and a lengthy poem based on the Proverbs.

Then suddenly my old friend Einar Arnfinnsson turned up in the yard at Bjarg; I had not set eye on him since we were at Reynistadur, and had heard little news of his travels for quite a while. As was to be expected, it was a joyful reunion and as soon as we began talking it became clear that a great turnabout had taken place in his fortunes.

He was now on his way from Hólar where he had been granted full reinstatement and absolution for his offence of begetting a child outside wedlock and he had been ordained as Deputy Vicar to his father back home in Hrútafjördur, and also given a letter promising him the office himself after the Archdeacon, who was becoming quite elderly.

My spirits lifted greatly to have Einar back near by. Our conversations ranged far and wide when we met, which was often.

Once when we met, Einar was on his way from a synod at Vídimýri, and he mentioned that he had spoken to the Bishop and that they had touched on my situation. He had the feeling that various old scores between us, including my scurrilous writings, were no longer uppermost in the Bishop's mind. Einar urged me to make every effort to ensure that those wounds would heal over. Then we would aim for me to become his Chaplain at Stadur when the moment arrived; such an office could undoubtedly serve me as a platform to another, great one in the course of time.

As I reflected upon this prospect, my old ambition and yearning to enter the ranks of scholars flared up within me again, since I felt my rightful place was certainly there, knowing myself to be so much more learned than most of the parish bumblers I ran into.

Einar spoke to the Bishop again when they met later, spoke well of me and said I was like a new man, and heaped praises on my many and good qualities that would go to waste if the present situation went on. Einar also claimed that the Bishop was in much lighter spirits than before, when the strain of his terrible Bible publication had weighed so heavily upon him.

In the end, I became preoccupied once more by resuming where I had left off, and for a while the prospects looked favourable. I knew examples of people who had suffered tribulations and punishment but regained their offices by reconciliation. This had been the case with Einar and the same was true of the Reverend Hallgrímur Pétursson. When I had stayed with him and his wife the year before, on my trip to the south for stockfish, he had been reconciled with Brynjólfur, the Bishop of Skálholt, been ordained there and made Vicar of Hvalsnes. Admittedly it was not a pleasant job, serving that mixture of over-bearing noblemen and appalling wretches who lived in the area, but it was a start anyway for someone who wanted to be something.

Hallgrímur told me with a laugh that his parishioners had said, when they heard about his ordination: 'They ordain all kinds of devils today!'

To which I found myself replying, 'All kinds of devils, yes, but just not me.'

ercifully I had little contact with the Sheriff from Thingeyrar and his son during my first years back in their district. The Sheriff did not think it was worth the bother to pursue me any longer, so ill and unstable and crushed as he had doubtless been told that I was. And as time went by and I began to recover, neither of us harassed nor approached the other, although we did catch sight of each other occasionally at assemblies or other gatherings.

By now, Sheriff Gudmundur was quite a way past the lightest side of life, in all the manifold meanings of that phrase. Over the years he became steadily more bloated, almost wondrously so, and in the end he could hardly support his own weight and could be carried only by the most powerful packhorses. He collected a whole team of such beasts of burden in order to be able to ride respectably to the Althing every summer. I imagine now how necessary and useful he would have found it to acquire if only one of the huge Danish horses that clatter around the streets and squares here – of course with a reinforced ladder included for the man of law to mount it.

Little love was said to be lost between Gudmundur and his son Thorkell. Maybe the Sheriff finally realized that his son's lax grip on his schooling was perhaps not entirely to be credited to my humble account.

What was certain was that Thorkell did not last for long back home at Thingeyrar when he finally left school. No one had much idea of what had become of him, but word went around that he had gone to the South to join a fishing boat. Some people said he had stayed on there and settled at Álftanes, entered the service of the Danes and ingratiated himself with them, since he put up with them making him do anything they ordered. It was said that he had made a considerable amount of money. Thorkell was supposed to be a close friend of the Governor, and rumours gradually spread that he enjoyed such backing from the Danes and had set his sights so high that he now said he would turn up his nose at a croft like the cloister at Thingeyrar even if it were offered to him on his father's death; so it seemed likely that this fat perk would slip from their family's grasp, since Gudmundur had no other son but Thorkell.

On my trips to fetch stockfish I made several inquiries about Thorkell and heard some things that bolstered many of the rumours back home about his whereabouts. No one in the South, however, would confirm that he was opposed to the idea of taking over his father's jurisdiction of the district and cloister lands in the course of time. Thorkell and I never ran across each other on those trips of mine, and I was not exactly eager to meet him either.

But no matter how things really were, whether or not Thorkell's ascendancy and prospects were an exaggeration, Sheriff Gudmundur did seem prepared to have to secure his family's future at the cloister by other means. And once again the one man appeared on the scene who was surely the least welcome guest my poor self could have wished for in those parts.

Since last crossing my path, Thorleifur Kortsson the tailor, the Sheriff's one-eyed nephew, had spent several years more under his uncle's wing in Hamburg, in order to go on perfecting himself in the tailor's trade. Then suddenly he returned home and stayed at Thingeyrar with his mother's brother. And as he stayed longer, it emerged that he had not gone there to sew clothes for the Sheriff, which would have been a mammoth task and best left to a sailmaker, but to study law and the ways of men of authority from his uncle. He was always around when the Sheriff was called out, at the Spring Assembly and elsewhere. He rode to the Althing with him, it was said, stood by and closely observed everything that went on; keeping his eye on things, as the jokers said.

If anyone had been wondering what was going on here, nobody was left in any doubt any more when Thorleifur Kortsson was appointed the Sheriff's Agent, that is to say legal official, of the Húnavatn district in spring 1646.

The most noticeable change in local legal proceedings with Thorleifur's arrival was that he took much more interest in sorcerers than Gudmundur had been accustomed to. Thorleifur did not make do with sentencing and burning those who were accused or charged; he also sought out alleged sorcerers and seemed to see them everywhere. Many people had to be on their guard.

I soon heard that Thorleifur was making inquiries about me. Clearly the idea that I practised the ancient arts was still uppermost in his thoughts after our earlier dealings, and I undoubtedly still had that kind of reputation. As before, I mostly had myself to blame for all those whisperings, since I could not resist the temptation to imply to certain people that I knew a thing or two; this proved invaluable for me when I went fishing and buying stockfish, where I invariably had to deal with all manner of riffraff. Nothing could beat a reputation for magic to keep brutes in their place. Often it did not take much: uneducated people needed only to hear a couple of words of Latin and immediately they took it to be a curse.

In the South-West I once met a man who was considered an exceptionally lucky fisherman and I bought from him more than once. It was said that his good luck was entirely brought about by an outstandingly mighty charm which he always muttered when he reached the fishing grounds, and then there was no question about it, he would fish well. He did not want to teach anyone the charm, saying it possessed such power that it was not for mere weaklings to tangle with.

Once when we were warming ourselves over a drink, that man and I, after making a deal for some fish, I managed all the same to get him to recite his charm to see if I could make out some of the words. Of course I assured him I was so ignorant that I could never remember such mighty lore, since I had also concealed from him that I had ever been to school. In the end he gave into my persuasions and began: *In*

113

principio creavit Deus caelum et terram, and proceeded to recite the first passages of Genesis in Latin, albeit somewhat distorted and garbled, which some malicious man of learning had taught him to recite parrot fashion as a magic formula.

I did not have the heart to tell that old man the truth, but found out when I went there the following summer that a clergyman had heard about his magic curse, and wanted to turn him from his evil ways. He adopted the same method as I had, and persuaded the old man to recite his charm while they warmed themselves with drink. But when the clergyman heard it, in his shock as much as embarrassment he told the old man the whole story, that his charm was the opening of the Holy Scriptures in Latin. And whatever the cause was, the result was that the old man felt his charm had lost all its power after that and he never recited it again. At the same time he stopped catching more fish than other people. Is it not always the case with what is called magic, that it is faith that moves mountains?

Knowing that this one-eyed bird of prey was hovering over me and feeling his shadow closing in on me, I took special pains not to give him the opportunity to strike at me a second time, and completely gave up implying to anyone that I could see past the end of my nose.

As it happened, it was in a different area that I got in the way of Thorleifur and his busybodying. My trade in spirits and tobacco soon came to irritate him enormously, not because he was gravely concerned that the law was being broken or that immorality and trouble were being visited on the children of the parish. No, above all the reason was that he did a roaring trade of his own back home in Thingeyrar, and could not bear the thought of anyone else coming near such lucrative business.

I was made patently aware of Thorleifur's longing for my downfall once when I was travelling back from the trading post at Höfdi and came face to face with him and his men. I greeted them as I moved out of their way, but he scarcely returned my greeting, only glaring at me as before with his single needle-eye. Then as they rode past he said, 'You schoult keep yourself in tcheck, Gusmundur. You are being votched.'

After that meeting I tried harder than ever to prevent Thorleifur from finding a chink in my armour. But in the end justice would be given the chance to bear down on me elsewhere.

Ever since my marriage proposal had been so evilly ruined by my enviers, I had not felt affection for any woman with the prospect of marriage, and did not entertain such ideas even though my mother would suggest every so often I should seek the hand of some farmer's daughter or other from Midfjördur who she considered a reasonable match at that time. I dispelled all such thoughts and tried instead as best I could to discipline and tame my body and direct my mind towards books and learning, whenever free time was available. Behind this lay my long determination once more to enter somehow the spiritual and scholarly path I had once set my mind on. I felt now that having a family and swarm of children to support would be a difficult obstacle to surmount on such a course. Once I had clinched a ministry, it would be an easy task to find a suitable lady.

However, my chastity could not avoid the occasional setbacks when it turned out to be true that

> Instinct may be swayed and strapped
> but never down the middle snapped.

Or, as Horace says in his first Epistle: *Naturam expellas furca licet usque recurrit*, which I versified as follows:

> Although you strain with might and main
> and nature from you banish,
> back it will come as strong again
> and never want to vanish.

116

I mean, on occasion I did happen to tumble into the beds of farm women when I was visiting or staying somewhere to teach children during the winters. And on my travels and journeys it sometimes came to pass, especially after gatherings where there was merriment and drinking, that light-hearted girls would loosen their garments in my honour up on a haystack or behind a hillock or in a cattleshed. On the rare occasions that this happened, I had the good fortune not to get any of them with child. But the repugnant act of adultery, namely lying with another man's wife – that I never allowed to befall me, never sought it nor took advantage of the opportunity if it arose.

Although I exercised every caution, it was eventually one such act of fornication that sufficed the authorities to deal me the blow that led at last to my apparent fate: to be forgotten until my dying day. A certain unfortunate girl by the name of Arnfríður Jónsdóttir, poor and destitute but sweet and kind-hearted, was more or less permanently resident at Bjarg at this time, although no records were kept of it. She was born in the West Fjords where reputedly all her family came from, but she had lost her mother while still a child and after that had spent time at various farms in different parts of the region with her father, who worked as a journeyman farmhand. When the famine struck they roamed the countryside as beggars until he died somewhere from cold and hardship. This was the situation she was in when she arrived at Bjarg, where my mother took her in, and she stayed with us for some while afterwards, almost like any other woman working on the farm. She looked after the cows and the ewes and other jobs that needed doing, and was rewarded with her keep. Some people knew she was staying with us, but no one bothered to make any fuss about it. Everyone had his own business to mind.

Arnfríður was in her early twenties and soon became a great source of happiness to me; no one could soothe me better if I was in poor spirits. It was mainly with songs and poetry that she entertained me. Her late father had been a fairly good poet and great performer of verse, for which he was welcomed in most of the places they had stayed during her youth. From him she had learned a vast store of all

117

kinds of poems, some of them very ancient, and had learned them from hearing him recite them, since she was illiterate.

She would entertain me for hours with her poems and all sorts of stories too, which she told well. But our many conversations on such matters inevitably led us to feel a certain love for each other, and those emotions increased little by little until at last they kindled carnal lust, although I tried for a long time to withstand it, wanting to preserve us from all such things. In the end we could not resist the temptation and I went to her bed every night afterwards that winter, and when spring came and then the height of summer we engaged in lovemaking whenever and wherever the opportunity presented itself.

It often occurred to me that we were tempting fate, but I dispelled such thoughts as the girl had become very dear to me. My mother was well aware of our lovemaking and doubtless had her own opinions about it, but she never mentioned that she disapproved, although this could never be the future mistress of the farm at Bjarg. Without a doubt she appreciated our relationship's effect of calming my temperament. In my dreams of spirituality, I too knew that no one would be considered a desirable clergyman who had chosen such a lowly person for his wife. I had never had any such thought in mind, although this changed later when the situation became desperate.

So I strove to preserve us from conceiving a child as I best knew how, and I recalled certain points from the Reverend Einar's teachings in the past about the look in the eyes, postures and positions and countless superstitions that he performed to prevent conception. I would have done better to have remembered how successful those plans turned out for him in the end!

Often I started out genuinely determined to practise the custom of Onan which Einar had so enthusiastically described and sometimes I managed to succeed in my plan during the early stage of our carnal relations, but as time went by it more frequently happened that when Frída and I were reaching the point where our ecstasy burst into full bloom, we failed in our resolve to tear ourselves apart in the manner that the noble Onan and his brother's widow had done when they made their sport.

For this I earned my just deserts. Just as I felt I was rapidly rebuilding the confidence of the highest authorities in me, something happened yet again that could only dash my hopes, and this time for once and for all.

By the spring of 1647 it was clear what was in the offing: Arnfríður was pregnant by me and soon her condition became obvious to everybody. She gave birth to a bouncing baby boy just before the end of the year. And thereby I saw my fate spread out before me. Clearly gloating, Sheriff's Agent Thorleifur Kortsson came to Bjarg and interrogated everyone about our relationship and the pregnancy in a humiliating fashion, though there was not actually anything to investigate since a full confession had been made. I did not disclaim the boy and it must have been perfectly obvious how his life had been kindled.

Arnfríður and I were summonsed to the spring assembly and sentenced to pay eighteen ells of cloth each for begetting a child out of wedlock, under the strictures of the Great Edict; this was valued at one thaler for each of us. But Arnfríður was also ordered to leave the district and return to her own part of the country, where she did not know a soul. Thorleifur humiliated her greatly with his words, reviling her and calling her an outright whore and harlot. His entire speech was in the very same vein I would soon attack when I began to write my *Discursus*. This same folly is predominant in the Bible that they published at Hólar, where the single word 'fornication' is used regardless of whether the Latin text says *scortatio* or *fornicatio*. Furthermore: *amica, concubina, conjunx, meretrix, scortum, fornicaria, prostibulum*, all these were rendered as 'fornicators' – heptonyms. But our language is not so impoverished as to be unable to find different terms for each of these. The word may be distinguished just as the deed is: lover, concubine, whore, harlot and mistress, *item* beloved. These are different concepts, not all fornicators and fornication.

In many parts of their Bible they have translated with the word 'fornicator' where they should talk of a 'harlot', and describe lustful and illicit acts which are nothing to do with an honourable female companion whom a man has human dealings with. Likewise the

119

promulgators of the Great Edict mix everything together and extrapolate gross whoredom and harlotry on to the straightforward act of conception. Even when a God-fearing man and a respectable woman are led astray into producing a child outside wedlock, in simple fornication.

I was outraged at hearing Thorleifur's monstrous words bearing down on my dear Frída and challenged his ruling about banishing her, saying that I intended to make her my wife, but he gave no quarter, she was to be sent away.

She had no longing herself to stay in the district after such treatment, so the outcome was that I was left behind licking my wounds, bereft of my woman and my son, humiliated by my worst adversary on yet another occasion, this time in the name of official law, namely the Great Edict, and my hopes for advancement were reduced to nothing into the bargain.

Around this time I felt myself being haunted by the same derangement that I had suffered before. After sentence had been passed and carried out and Frída had vanished with the child, whom I have never seen or heard of since and do not even know to this day whether is dead or alive, I was beset by intense depression and began to fear for a while that I might once again plunge into the madness that had previously seized me for half a year and left me completely bedridden.

So to replenish myself I hurried off to see my old friend Einar at Stadur. We talked about many things and repeatedly returned to the outrageous legislation that we had both now fallen foul of, that is to say the Great Edict. We sat there well into the night, trying to outwit each other in finding arguments against this lawlessness.

Feeling that I was finding better arguments than he could, Einar suggested that we should turn this into a rhetorical exercise as we had done at school in the old days. I should continue to criticize the edict, and he would counter my arguments. We did so, creating a huge and entertaining storm about a highly unentertaining subject, but could not agree which of us had come off the better. So the idea arose that we should ask for a ruling on the matter, and we more or less took for granted that no one would be better qualified to arbitrate than our old friend and mentor, the Reverend Arngrímur the Learned, who was now fairly advanced in years and in failing health.

We took some horses at once and a barrel of spirit to drink on the way, and galloped off, even though it was the middle of the night. We reached Melstadur in the early hours of the morning, were received with honour and immediately began putting our case to Arngrímur, for and against, noisily and rowdily since we had got thoroughly drunk on the journey. But we soon realized that the aged Archdeacon could scarcely hear a thing any more and had deteriorated sharply in a short time, and it made little difference even when he put two brass trumpets to his ears. So we had to shout our arguments and counter-arguments at him, but Arngrímur began to grow tired and proposed that we should try instead to write down what we had to say about the Great Edict, then send it to him to read over so that he could judge the matter.

This seemed a fine piece of advice to us, and Arngrímur stood up immediately and hobbled over to fetch some fine paper which he gave me for the purpose. We turned to discussing lighter matters and stayed there for most of the day, then our thoughts turned to our homes again and we departed.

Over the period that ensued I saved myself from another bout of sickness by starting to write at once, writing at a furious pace for a few weeks. And I immediately felt that although we had ventured on this as on a schoolboys' trivial prank, I did not consider it a mere frippery once I committed all my arguments to paper and supported them with numerous examples from the Holy Scriptures and other books. My mind was completely preoccupied with everything put forward there.

Then I sent my writings to the Reverend Arngrímur in the form of a private letter, to give him the chance to correct my *Discursus*. And on closer examination, his request to undertake this writing was equivalent to an order from him, the most learned scholar and most venerable old man in Iceland, since he had sworn that my pamphlet would not be circulated or shown to anyone else. Had I held back and not committed anything to writing to send him after such a promise, that could have been seen as a gesture of distrust towards the honourable old man.

Some time later I received a letter from the Reverend Arngrímur thanking me for my writings and saying that I had done him more than a small favour with my comments on the Great Edict. He said he echoed Socrates' words: 'What I have understood is sensible; may the same be true of that which I have not understood.'

The reason for this was that a number of scribal errors in my text had prevented him from understanding a few points entirely when he read them. He condemned nothing in any of my arguments nor expressed his disapproval of them, but said that at present he did not want to advocate the opinions I presented there. He said he wanted to discuss them better with us at his leisure and examine more closely to what extent they were untenable.

Some of his thoughts he had begun to scribble down in the margin of my pamphlet, but had little time for this task. Only a few days later, on the twenty-seventh day of June, *anno domini* 1648, he died, replete with life, only two weeks after receiving my writings.

Hearing of this, I went straight over to Melstadur to pay my respects to the bereaved, and took care to retrieve my essay to prevent it from entering the wrong hands. The Reverend Einar was there too, and he took on himself to assist Mistress Sigrídur, Arngrímur's widow, with various tasks that needed to be attended to concerning the death and funeral. He asked me for the essay and took it back to Stadur to examine it, then returned it not long afterwards with an unclear inscription and some scribblings in the margin, saying he did not feel capable of countering my arguments in defiance of his own feelings, that would be easier to handle in torrents of spoken abuse than individually in writing. I kept the essay for a while and guarded it like the apple of my eye from the prying of malicious people.

But I had already committed one unfortunate blunder, when the increasing relish for drink and tobacco that had come upon me with redoubled vigour after Frída's departure had led me into temptation and I had been incautious, as would soon emerge with horrendous consequences.

Early in the spring while I was energetically at work composing my *Discursus*, before I sent it to the Reverend Arngrímur, I had been seized by a longing for tobacco and spirits. I took a horse and rode off without anyone missing me, since I no longer paid attention to anything but my writing. I had taken my essay with me, continually pondering over it, and whenever the chance arose I corrected and improved the occasional point in my arguments. I also took various poems of mine to recite at places where I stayed, including my *Ballads* and *Metrical Key* and likewise some fragments based on the Proverbs. I called at many farms where I had friends and knew there was a chance of tobacco or spirits, but nothing was to be had anywhere; it was all finished after the winter. I went from one farm to the next around the whole of Vatnsnes peninsula, but unfortunately seldom received anything to smoke or drink for my pains, however much poetry I recited. Most people were waiting for the first ship to arrive that spring, as I was too.

On the way back I made a diversion which led me within sight of Thingeyrar, and for a while I pondered whether I dared to go there and see the deacon, who was a good friend of mine. Eventually my pride prevented me from doing so, since I knew that Thorleifur Kortsson would hear of it and gloat over the knowledge that I had run out of supplies. So I turned back and decided to go straight home, copy out the final draft of my work and send it at the first opportunity to the Reverend Arngrímur as I had promised.

Riding up towards the farm called Stóraborg I suddenly saw in the distance, coming down the path towards me, a person who, as far as I could tell, was a complete stranger. As we approached each other, curiously enough, the man clearly seemed to recognize me and headed straight towards me with his arms stretched out wide in welcome, as if he had chanced on one of his oldest and best friends or relatives. What knocked me flat, however, was that judging from what he said he was apparently none other than Thorkell Gudmundsson. I had dismounted and fallen into his arms before I had the chance to decide how to react to him.

I had not set eyes on Thorkell since around the time I had left school some ten years before, had heard little about him and to tell the truth had not missed him. Occasionally I could not avoid thinking about the way everything might have turned out if the episode with the silver spoons had never arisen. Hadn't one thing led to another in my misfortunes and wasn't this the foundation of everything that had since turned out to my disfavour and provoked the authorities against me when the stakes were highest?

But now he was standing there like a completely new man, polite and pleasant and almost cheerful in disposition, slim and muscular and apparently not bearing the slightest resemblance to his father or the fat pock-faced youth who had made my life a misery at Hólar. He said that he had bought the land at Stóraborg and was busy building a house there and settling in. He invited me to go there and stay as his guest, so that we could make a splendid celebration and recall our 'happy old schooldays', as he suddenly called them.

The thought crossed my mind that had noble Ovid still been alive and been in Iceland, he could have found Thorkell's transformation an ideal subject to work on for another of his *Metamorphoses*. I also happened to drop my guard completely and felt that such a metamorphosis was an interesting enough reason to accepted his generous offer. Besides which I was hungry and tired and, naturally, no less desperate for tobacco and spirits, goods that such a wealthy man surely had in abundance. This turned out to be the case, for we had hardly sat down in Thorkell's home before he poured me a glass of spirit and made sure that it was always full to the brim, no matter how often I emptied it.

In brief, this was his story since we last met. After his hopes were dashed at Hólar, as time went by he felt the most convenient thing to do was to remove himself from the presence of his father, the Sheriff. He was convinced that the old man would soon realize it was more than Gudmundur Andrésson's alleged sorcery that had caused his misfortune and poor footing as he trod the path to learning. So Thorkell had been delighted to head south and join a fishing boat. He ended up at Álftanes and was in the service of the Danes during the summers, ingratiated himself with them, and said that he never kept them waiting when they asked him to do anything. He earned plenty and was soon a wealthy man, in both land and money.

He had hardly kept in touch with his father over these years, he said, since a coldness had developed between them and became a full enmity which still prevailed, after it emerged that the Sheriff intended to grant Thorleifur Kortsson the power and authority that Thorkell considered himself rightful heir to. He chose the most sarcastic words about his relative, that one-eyed tailor, whom he had once held in such great respect.

Given the course that events had taken, he had intended until very recently to settle down in the south and was involved with a young widow in Álftanes, attractive and wealthy but temperamental and headstrong. But around the same time he became overfriendly with a female relative of the Governor himself, and when the widow found out she vowed to kill the Danish girl whom he prized more highly than herself, then to kill him afterwards.

Not long afterwards the widow died, Thorkell said, and the strange thing was that the body vanished the first night it was laid out to rest. Then the night after that the Danish girl at Bessastadir succumbed to such a mighty illness that she was racked with constant pain, and within three nights she too had died in terrible agony.

After that, Thorkell said he no longer felt safe in the South, so he had decided to buy some land close to Thingeyrar and moved back there, where he could also keep a closer watch on his family, to make sure they did not disinherit him and cut him off completely. He thought he could possibly pose more of a threat to them at this place.

That was his story and I swallowed every word of it, completely forgetting to ask him whether he didn't have just as much cause up north to fear the plot that the widow was supposed to have made against his own life, which in retrospect was an obvious flaw in his tale. But I paid no heed to ask anything of this sort, for Thorkell had us served with delicacies all the while he told his story, and when the barrel of spirits ran out a new one was brought out from one of the sheds. So I was thoroughly drunk when my turn came around to repay the favour and tell him my story since we had last met.

When I mentioned how the start of my tribulations could be traced back to Thorkell's own schoolboy pranks, his eyes filled with tears of remorse, even though I handled his part in the matter diplomatically. And at the point where my story ended with me sentenced as a fornicator, deprived of my woman and my child, he broke into a fit of howling and sobbing and was almost inconsolable for long afterwards, and did not calm down until I produced my writings and poems and began reciting to him.

All of a sudden I had produced my *Discursus* in its entirety and started reading aloud from it to my dear host. The last thing I remember before the bird of oblivion sank its claws into my shoulders was Thorkell being enraptured by my insights and heaping such praise on my inquiry that I swelled up and promised him, without checking myself, that he might copy out the essay. And when he went on to ask if he could keep two of the twenty original pages in my own hand, I thought it not only the right and obvious thing to do, but in fact the highest of honours.

The next day I woke up fairly late and was quite shocked when I remembered what I had promised. I became even more pensive when I got up and came across one of Thorkell's lackeys, a cross-eyed character with a club foot, sitting at a table and finishing copying out my manuscript. Then Thorkell came into the room with a jug full of spirit and filled my glass to the brim, and said he was disappointed when I mentioned that I had to be hurrying on my way.

I received my essay again, apart from two pages, and now there was nothing for me to do but to exact an exceedingly solemn promise from my new-found good friend that he would never show anyone my writings about the Great Edict without my permission, and I described to him in detail the danger it could pose to me.

I recovered well after drinking the spirits and hearing Thorkell's oath of confidentiality, then went on my way back to Bjarg.

N ot many days after I had sent my completed essay to the Reverend Arngrímur, I received from my friend the Deacon of Thingeyrar what I thought was disturbing news, that Thorkell and his father had been reconciled. They had agreed that Thorkell should be granted the authority of Sheriff's Agent and in Húnavatn district, then assume all his father's powers after his day, if this could be arranged. Thorleifur Kortsson, on the other hand, had been assigned the district of Ísafjördur where he would soon become an Agent too. It was said that he was delighted at this transfer and looked forward to tackling all the sorcerers who had been left in peace to practise their activities in that part of the country for far too long. The Deacon reported that Thorleifur had been in regular contact by letter with little Páll Björnsson, who had returned from university abroad several years before and been granted the benefice of Selárdalur in Arnarfjördur in the West Fjords. He was said to be enormously learned by now, but also twice as zealous as ever against those he alleged to practise witchcraft, who were not few in number.

On first impression it might be thought that I should welcome the fact that Thorleifur had left and my new-found special friend Thorkell would assume authority in the district. Yet I doubted that I could trust this boded well for me. My fear proved well founded. It was Thorkell who had made the most effort to appease the old man. And one of the means he used to appear saintly in his eyes was, according to the Deacon, the distorted and garbled copy of my *Discursus* that the rogue had acquired from me with his treacherous and conniving ways. Thorkell had actually forced his father, against his will, to accept the essay, which the old man had simply passed off in advance, without even having read it, as mere nonsense if it came from a madman like me.

But once he had read it he was very much shaken and flew into a rage, claiming that it made a mockery of his own legal knowledge and the wisdom of past generations, and he stormed around resolving that I would suffer for it in the end.

So I started to fear greatly for my safety when I heard this described in such terms, and I soon received confirmation too that the father and son had in fact been reconciled: I noticed that they rode together to the Althing. While they were away I hurriedly wrote a letter to Sheriff Gudmundur, pleading as humbly as I possibly could, and had it delivered at once to Thingeyrar so that it would be waiting for him when he returned after the Althing.

In the letter I tried to make clear what it was that I had actually written, *item* that I did not acknowledge as my own the piece of writing they had in their hands. If, on the other hand, he desired to examine the ungarbled version, he could obtain it from the Reverend Arngrímur. I said I was willing to undergo an investigation which was based on the correct contents of the essay and would take these circumstances fairly into account.

I never received any reply to my overture; the Sheriff showed me no such courtesy, but I did hear that he had called me a 'ness-dweller', using the Danish phrase for an arrogant person, for my audacity in rummaging around and wanting to change what past generations and government officials had prescribed. I reacted angrily and went around telling people that I had not been brought up on any ness and did not deserve such a patronymic, nor had I learned the little that I knew on a ness or its like-ness like Sheriff Gudmundur.

He never made a search for the original essay, but when he and his son returned from the Althing they began circulating the garbled version of it as an anonymous lampoon unquestionably attributed to me. It was passed around in this way from one person to the next, to my denigration. So I must surely ask which of us was more enthusiastic about spreading the corruptive heresy that it contained. Were they, or I?

Likewise the fact that I had referred to the Reverend Arngrímur in my letter to the Sheriff rebounded on me, quite contrary to my intention in naming him. When they returned from the Althing, Arngrímur was dead, and they soon spread the rumour that his deep shock at my awful tract had played its part in cutting short his life.

At all this I grew very apprehensive and lay low, deciding to put my essay to one side until I saw what they were aiming at by circulating their own garbled version of it. Then I soon heard that they had done the same thing at the Althing, and even presented my alleged writings to Bishop Thorlákur with a request that he and the Rector of the school should write a denunciation of it.

The Bishop was said to be furious at my audacity and the immoral influences that I wanted to call on everyone in Iceland. I knew myself that one sentence of mine irritated him more than any other. I had shamefully put forward the following example in defence of respectable fornication. 'It is not long since a man with five children married a bishop's daughter, and became a bishop's father.' Everyone knew, and no one better than he did, that I could be referring only to his own father, Skúli Einarsson from Eiríksstadir.

As autumn approached I talked the matter over in detail with my close friends and family, and most of them thought the Bishop and Sheriffs were furious enough to summons me to the Althing the following year and even have me condemned to death for the outrage of which they considered me guilty.

We decided that my best chance of defending myself would be to pre-empt Their Lordships and go straight to the one Lordship who was higher in rank than them all, namely the King himself. By referring my case directly to him, there would be more chance of my securing just treatment, since he would be able to hear my own arguments and not the accusations made by the Bishop and Sheriff and their men, and I could allow the King to interpret my own essay rather than their abortion of it.

The last ship that autumn would soon be leaving the trading post at Höfdi, so it was decided that I should ride there as quickly as possible, secure myself a passage and make arrangements with the

130

crew, and in the meanwhile my mother, the Reverend Einar and other wellwishers of mine, including Arngrímur's widow Sigrídur, would gather together the goods I needed for the journey so that I could pay for the passage and have enough to live on at first when I arrived in Denmark. Einar was also going to write a letter to the learned Doctor Ole Worm, to whom he had written before on behalf of Mistress Sigrídur, reporting Arngrímur's death and enclosing various lore that he knew the Doctor was trying to seek out. In the same letter he had asked the Doctor to do what he could to assist Thorkell Arngrímsson, the couple's eldest son, who was studying at the university, in securing a letter promising him the benefice at Melstadur, so that the widow with her young children would not be forced to leave at the end of her year's grace.

It was known that Doctor Worm eagerly pursued ancient Icelandic lore but could not read Icelandic himself, and many a young Icelandic student had benefited from doing scholarly work for him. Einar wrote me a fine reference and set particular store by describing my proficiency in the runes, since in his opinion it was about time that such knowledge served me with some other purpose than accusations of sorcery. If everything turned out as planned, Doctor Worm ought to be able to act as a powerful supporter in my dealings with the King, and likewise, he hoped, to assist me in making a living during the winter. Perhaps, at last, I would encounter good fortune in another country.

Everything seemed settled and it was with a happy heart that I hurried off northwards to the trading post at Höfdi. I went aboard a ship and was taken well with the promise of a passage, but unfortunately it was too early to rejoice that Lady Luck had granted me her favours at last. My baggage arrived so late that I missed it, the captain would not agree to wait any longer and I was left stranded. When Einar's men finally arrived with the horses on which my goods and provisions were loaded, the sails of the ship were still visible far on the horizon, but hopelessly beyond reach except for a bird on the wing.

After this there was nothing else for me to do but to turn back home and return what I had been sent to its respective owners with my best thanks. I kept Einar's letter to Doctor Worm, hoping that it would come in useful for me, if only later.

I never found out whether many people had heard about my plan, but asked Einar's men and all the others who knew about it to keep the matter quiet, since I knew that my enemies would turn it to their advantage and claim that I was trying to flee, thereby proving my fear of my own alleged ill-fated deed.

I spent that winter at Bjarg and little of note happened. I heard nothing from my adversaries, they did not harass me at all and I did not know anything of them until once just after Christmas, when I ran into Thorkell. I asked him whether he felt he had acted nobly in circulating a tract in my name, and he was lost for a reply. And when I pressed him, he admitted that he had promised me not to make public any of the material that I had permitted him to take.

I said that he had distributed my essay under false pretences and credited me with things which I had never written, said nor meant – or did he have any evidence to the contrary?

He said that my own manuscript could serve as evidence, in so far as it matched his. Then I laughed and said that he could not be sure it was still around. He excused himself, then said that his father had gained hold of the manuscript by force.

'You're lying, damn you,' I said then, 'but if this were true, your father would have done himself and you more damage than me, by circulating it in the way I have heard. Admittedly I laid that egg, but you have hatched out a chicken that does not resemble it in the slightest. What your scribe has written down is not the least bit my business until you swear to your words on oath.'

hen spring approached, in the present year of 1649, every day I fully expected to be summonsed to the Althing. This did not happen, however, and when the time for the Assembly came around I felt certain that it would not, and I even went so far as to hope that my exchange with Thorkell had served to detract my persecutors.

It also became clear in the spring that the Althing in the summer would involve many more noteworthy events than some poor farmer's scribblings. A schooner had arrived for the King's Agent at Bessastadir with a letter from the newly crowned King, Fredrik the Third, and another from the new Governor, Henrik Bjelke. They wrote to both Bishops, to the Lawspeakers, and then to the Sheriffs in each district, ordering them to arrange for the common people to swear their loyalty and true service to the new King. In confirmation, oaths would be taken at the Althing, and everyone expected it to be an occasion of great ceremony.

In this frame of mind I set off alone to buy stockfish in the South about the same time as the Althing, but kept a low profile. I took my normal route and had plenty of success in securing fish, offering mainly woollen gloves and homespun cloth in exchange. Afterwards I stayed one night at Hvalsnes with the Reverend Hallgrímur and his wife Gudrídur, whom it was very enjoyable to meet.

On the way from there I did not think it was too risky to travel quite close to Thingvellir, but shortly before I reached the Nordling-avad fording point over the river Öxará, I happened to ride into a group of men on their way to the Althing who were resting their horses by the wayside. Travelling there, with his men, was the wise and honourable Lawspeaker Árni Oddsson. In his party were several men who knew me from Hólar and pointed me out to him, and I realized how well known I had become through the actions of my enemies when he recognized me at once and said, 'So you are this Gudmundur who has challenged all the authorities of this country, Sheriffs and the Bishop and King alike. You're a surprisingly bold character, though you don't cut a very impressive figure. But what do you think will become of you, my friend, when you are taken before the Governor for protesting against the laws of the land? Because it is said that he wants to arrest you. I shall neither judge nor condemn your writings, that is not for me to do, nor do I have any say in your affairs. Some wise men I know praise your cleverness and learning. But my personal advice to you is to watch yourself as closely as you can.'

I tried to answer boldly without seeming arrogant, since the Lawspeaker's attitude had been completely amicable. I played down my challenge to the supreme authorities and said quite truthfully that only two clergymen had seen my essay besides myself, since it was never intended for the eyes of anyone but my friends. Other people than myself had circulated it, in fact in such a garbled form that I did not want to ac knowledge it as my own.

'Furthermore,' I added, 'I cannot understand why it is such a challenge to Their Lordships if I point out what I think is superior to them, namely the word of the Lord Himself as it appears in the Holy Scriptures and interpretations of the most noteworthy scholars.'

'And he's in closer contact with you than with the King and the Bishop?' the Lawspeaker asked, to which I replied that the Lord did not look to a man's rank.

Then I said I would continue on my way home, not having been summonsed. But for safety's sake I wrote a letter there and then and asked Árni, when he went to the Althing, to give it to his son-in-law, Archdeacon Thórdur Jónsson from Hítardalur, whom I had met the previous winter. I considered him a worthy man and likely to agree with me on many points judging by our earlier acquaintance. I asked

Thórdur in my note whether he would be my representative and spokesman *vis-à-vis* the Governor and his entourage if I were charged. I asked him to present the following statement to them.

'I have not issued any pamphlet, but the one for which I am charged is a forgery and unknown to me. But if you insist on my producing the one which I really wrote – although it was only one side of a private dialogue – and though I am now proceeding home (since no one has summonsed me to trial) I am quite willing if called on to accompany you to the Episcopal Seat or the Althing.'

Then I bade farewell to the Lawspeaker and his entourage and continued on my way towards Kaldidalur valley. Late in the evening I found myself a place to lie down for the night on a grassy slope where travellers rest their horses before heading for the interior. I leapt from the back of my horse and packed the fish carefully on the ground, wrapped myself up in some canvas and fell asleep in the open air, in mild and beautiful weather.

owards noon the next day, at the foot of the slope, I prepared to continue my journey. My horses had not roamed far and I was quick to round them up. I strapped the fish on to them and secured everything, skinned one of the fish and ate my fill from it, washing it down with water from a brook. Then I mounted my horse and before I knew it I was leading my horses in caravan up the track to where rock and boulders took over.

When I had almost reached the cairn that marked the trail at the top, I took one of my regular glances over my shoulder and noticed a small band of men riding after me at quite a gallop. One of the riders led the party with his legs bouncing all over the place, and the others followed close behind. I was immediately seized with a dark foreboding that these men felt they had some unfinished business with me, otherwise they would not have been in such a hurry. But here I simply had to accept my fate, I had no escape route at this place in the middle of the barren landscape. Besides which it would not have improved matters for me to flee like a common thief, that could only testify to bad conscience, but God knew that mine was clear. So I continued on my way and paid no heed to my pursuers, if that is what they were, but continued to thread my way up the rocky trail.

When the riders drew closer, however, my fears turned out to be right: they felt they had some business with me. The leader, huge as a demi-troll, started calling out to me through the clattering of hoofs, in a very gruff voice 'Stop, Gvendur, in the King's name, stop.'

Only then, and not before, did I dismount and wait for what was destined to happen. I was astonished when they rode up to me and I recognized their leader. It was Hallgrímur Halldórsson, gentleman farmer from Víðimýri in Skagafjördur, the son of the late Halldór Ólafsson, Lawspeaker, and therefore brother-in-law of Brynjólfur Sveinsson, Bishop of Skálholt, who was married to Hallgrímur's sister, Margrét. Hallgrímur was known throughout Skagafjördur as an overbearing and influential character and a braggart, who invariably bullied lowly people – not a popular man. I found it hard to understand how he could claim to act in the King's name, or by what miracle he had become a kind of honorary dogsbody for the authorities, if not their executioner, though the reason later became clear.

By now they were right upon me and even though I had already halted long before, Hallgrímur screamed to me again to stop in the King's name.

I answered him right back, wanting to show him that I did not hold him in the slightest fear: 'I didn't know they'd made you King, Grímsi, even though you think you can boss around a few peasants up in the North.'

I had heard rumours about his overbearing treatment of people of lower rank, but had no idea that I could rub him up the wrong way so terribly by referring to it. Hallgrímur turned crimson with rage and rained down blows on me with his whip, shouting to his men as he did so, 'Grab the rascal, lads.'

The others were already right up close to me, and leapt off their horses and attacked me violently and noisily while Hallgrímur yelled out from horseback some kind of rigmarole that I was hereby arrested in the King's name to be taken to the Althing at the demand of the supreme authorities of Iceland.

I protested vociferously, demanding to see papers to prove it, and said they were guilty of kidnapping me.

Laughing, Hallgrímur said I didn't know how to use paper properly. Then his men took out a huge rope and tied me up tight, keeping one end loose, and rode off dragging me along behind them. I had to run, but after I had fallen over twice and been dragged a short way along the ground they relented and slowed their pace.

I had received some scratches from being manhandled, but far worse was the way they seized me and left me completely destitute. My horses, fish and luggage, this was all left behind unattended, easy prey for ravens and vagrants, and Hallgrímur flatly refused to entertain the idea of doing anything else with them. He laughed at me and told me to keep my mouth shut when I demanded to be allowed to have the horses with me to hand over to one of my acquaintances at the Althing. So I had nothing with me but the rags I was wearing and Apuleius' *Golden Ass* in a little pouch inside my clothes.

They lugged me off to the Althing like this and I soon became exhausted, even though we were not travelling very fast. The fun had started to wear off, so eventually Hallgrímur ordered one of the men riding with him to carry me like a sack in front of him across the horse's back. Then we set off at a gallop, with them stopping every so often to refresh themselves with a nip of spirits, which I was never offered.

As we approached Thingvellir and could see the crowd in the distance, Hallgrímur ordered them to throw me off the horse's back again and they galloped into the court area with me continually stumbling over the rope, though fortunately I managed to avoid falling. It had clearly been Hallgrímur's plan to make quite a showy entrance, so that no one there could fail to notice us. It remained a mystery to me how such a noble-born man could expect to gain in stature from arresting a wretch like me.

But our arrival aroused much less attention than planned, even though the crowd was the largest ever heard of at the Althing. Instead, all eyes were focused on an impressive booth that had been set up on an islet in the river, hugely long and wide, with beams and crossbeams and rafters and partly clad with homespun. Speeches were being made there and everyone who was anyone was inside, while only children, poor women and idiots were there to notice Hallgrímur and his men when they galloped in brandishing their prey.

Hallgrímur cursed. Then they all dismounted and he sent one of his men off with the horses and ordered the other two to guard me carefully until it was decided what to do with me. He forced his way through the crowd, punching and shoving to get closer to the worthier men who filled the great booth or were standing right outside it. There was the vague sound of guttural Latin which soon stopped and turned into Danish. It was the King's Secretary, Gabriel Akkeley, who was speaking; he had come to Iceland to take the oath to the King from the people. I was too far away to be able to make out any words clearly. At the end of the speech, Bishop Thorlákur and Bishop Brynjólfur spoke in Latin for the scholars, and the Lawspeakers Árni and Magnús in Icelandic for the common people.

After this the bells were rung to announce the opening of the court, and the noblemen left the booth in procession, with Governor Bjelke leading the way with the King's Secretary, then the Bishops and Lawspeakers, then everyone else in order of rank. Then the oaths were taken, beginning with both Bishops who genuflected and raised their fingers on the central platform on the west side of the court. Brynjólfur went ahead of Thorlákur; then came the scholars, all the Archdeacons and the two clergymen from each diocese. I noticed Hallgrímur Pétursson there, wearing his cassock, among their ranks.

Next it was the turn of the laity who pledged their oaths in the same manner on their knees inside the boundaries of the court. First the two Lawspeakers, then the Sheriffs. There I saw Gudmundur Hákonarson fall to his knees so that the earth shook, and it took five men to hold under each of his armpits to get him back to his feet. After this it was the turn of the court judges, and finally two landholding farmers from each district, elected for this duty by the people, knelt in allegiance to the authorities.

I did not manage to follow the whole proceedings to the end, however, since Hallgrímur Halldórsson reappeared in grand style and ordered his men to take me away and put me in a tumbledown booth that belonged to the people from Hólar. All of this was at the command of Bishop Thorlákur; Hallgrímur had managed to pass on messages to him between the ceremonies on the islet and in the court.

So I was led up into what was left of the booth, crammed under a wall there and tied by my hands and feet, with one of the lads left behind to guard me, sitting on the wall. As it happened they just finished cramming me in there at the very moment that a triple cannon salute was fired down on the plains to mark the conclusion of the oath-taking.

After that the routine Assembly business began. I could not see what was happening, but every so often I wheedled out of the lad what was going on as far as he could tell from that distance. I found it chilly and monotonous being huddled up there in that hovel, without anything to refresh myself and ignored by everyone. The worst thing, however, was expecting at any time to be taken off and led for judgment by Their Lordships. Though I could not understand how such lawlessness could be performed, since I had not been charged with anything at all. But such men of authority, of course, did not need to ask questions about lawful procedures.

No one came to see me, which saddened me since I knew many of my friends were present at the Althing and was sure that word of my arrival would quickly spread. I felt my solitude sorely then.

The evening passed and night came, and it took me a long time to fall asleep in such a cold and hungry state, but I managed to doze off in the end after my guards had felt a little sorry for me, given me a sheepskin and blanket and handed me a jug of sour whey to drink and some dried fish to gnaw at. I slept in snatches through the night, woken intermittently by the sound of carousing and merrymaking coming up from the plains, shrieking and laughter, as many people had opted not to go to bed in the bright northern night.

he next day passed in the same way. I lay alone shivering in the tumbledown booth while people went about their duties at the Althing. I could hear echoes and snatches of their chattering and bickering every so often, but could not make out any words clearly. I had little idea of what was going on, but every second I expected to be lugged off and have my case heard, which none the less did not happen. If I tried to recite verse to myself to warm my body and console my mind, my guard would huffily order me to shut up.

It was unlike the prison where I am interred now in this tower, although in both places I suffered pain, hunger and harsh treatment. I experienced another thing which was the same by the Öxará and in the Blue Tower, that is to say being forgotten by everyone and not considered worth speaking to. But the difference is that here I yearn for this oblivion to come to an end and for fate to take its course, while in the tumbledown booth by the Öxará I hoped for the opposite, that the authorities would not remember about me until it was too late, when the Althing was over, which I thought could prove to be my salvation.

The whole day passed and when evening came I heard the sounding of trumpets and beating of drums, whereupon my guard finally pronounced that the Althing was being dissolved, after which a splendid feast would be held at the invitation of the Governor, the most magnificent ever to be held in Iceland. There was to be something for everyone, including the common people, at least a few crumbs and drops from Their Lordships' tables. My guard looked forward eagerly to that, since he was tired and bored at watching over me and was waiting for someone to come and relieve him.

That person came at last and turned out to be someone from Hólar, an old acquaintance of mine: old Pétur Gudmundsson, the relative of the court at Hólar who for most of the time had been the bellringer and errand-runner, and the father of my friend Hallgrímur Pétursson, Vicar at Hvalsnes.

Pétur was fairly grumpy about being assigned this job when such a ceremony was taking place, but he had been given a promise that he would be sent some of the delicacies and perhaps a drop to wash them down with. I thought Pétur was a great improvement, being more talkative than his predecessor and never trying to be condescending towards me despite his higher rank.

None the less, he could not give any answers about the fate that was in store for me, so I had to wallow in uncertainty. But when, filling with hope, I asked whether he thought they had forgotten all about me, he said the only thing he could assure me of was that they had not, because the Bishop always flared up until he glowed with rage at the mention of my name, and he had strictly forbidden everyone to go and see me or have any other dealings with me. Which many people had wanted, Pétur said, passing on special greetings from Björn from Skardsá and other friends of mine.

Pétur said that Bishop Thorlákur had ingratiated himself particularly well with the new Governor, Captain Bjelke. They were as thick as thieves and the Captain had already accepted the Bishop's invitation to go straight to Hólar at the end of the Althing.

Another story Pétur had to tell was that Hallgrímur Halldórsson was generally not considered to have grown in stature by his ignoble deed of setting off to capture me, and it was said that his brother-in-law, Bishop Brynjólfur, was enraged at him for his part in the expedition.

Pétur also knew the answer to what I had been pondering so intensely, the explanation for the petty King's notion that he would benefit from chasing a helpless crofter halfway up a mountain.

What had happened was that, as I knew before, Hallgrímur from Vídimýri had for a long time bullied the King's tenants in the vicinity of his farm in Skagafjördur, treating them overbearingly and haughtily. In the end some of those lowly farmers could stand it no more, and had presented a series of charges to the authorities against Hallgrímur for his brutality. And since a new Governor was expected and Hallgrímur had no idea of his character and possible reaction to such complaints, and fearing that he might come off second best at the Althing, he thought the safest course of action would be to visit the Governor, present his case and ingratiate himself with him before the Althing began.

So he had set off early for the Althing with his men, but first of all headed straight for the Governor's residence at Bessastadir, aiming to make a triumphal journey but which instead turned out to be a huge disgrace. Pétur knew the episode in detail, having heard it recounted by someone who had been present.

Hallgrímur and his men had ridden up to Bessastadir and pitched their tents on the field near by, which was not entirely a flawless exercise since they were naturally all fairly inebriated after the journey. The Governor, apparently, had been taking a stroll outside the hall and witnessed the way they rode up and went about pitching their tents, and concluded that they were not desirable company. He ordered his men to drive that rabble away. The locals hesitated about it when they went to the tents and recognized Hallgrímur, familiar as they were with his ruthlessness and brutality. The Steward tried to explain to the Governor what the mission of the man from Skaga-fjördur was, and that he was unlikely to move away even if asked to. But the Governor said it was fitting to teach such peasants how to behave in front of their superiors, and that it was quite sufficient for him to present his defence at the Althing, where they would meet anyway.

Then the Governor was told that this peasant, as he called him, was in fact the most noble of men, the son of the late Lawspeaker and brother-in-law of no less a man than Brynjólfur, Bishop of Skálholt, so that it was hardly fitting to drive him away like a mere dog. The Governor calmed down and said the best thing for him then would be to meet this specimen of true Icelandic aristocracy, and he had Hallgrímur invited in to table, for it happened that dinner was just about to be served.

Completely unaware of the background and this exchange, Hallgrímur regarded the invitation as a straightforward testimony to the Governor's desire to show him the highest honour. He gloated in the conviction that his problems were virtually settled, since the authorities had immediately proved so friendly and obliging. So he wore quite a proud look on his face when he said goodbye to his men and stomped off to knock on the door to the hall.

But something quite different awaited him. At table, the Governor immediately mentioned the charges brought by his tenants, and he gave the impression of being very well informed about the entire matter. He soon began speaking sharply and asked Hallgrímur firmly what he meant by such behaviour.

At first, Hallgrímur was caught off balance by these accusations, which were not exactly what he had expected. As usual he lost his temper, erupted, lost control of himself and forgot where he was, surely imagining he was back home in Skagafjördur, and he set out to brush off the Governor's admonitions with brute force. He answered him boldly at first, then suddenly felt he was making little headway and began using strong words in his bad Danish, augmenting it with curses in his own language, so abusive that the Icelanders present were outraged, and the Danes could at least understand the tone and catch the spirit of what he was saying. Hallgrímur said he had a much better idea than any Dane of the treatment that ought to be handed out to peasants in Skagafjördur who were continually being arrogant and insolent to their superiors.

The Governor answered calmly that the law was the law, and the King had to protect his tenants against injustice. At which Hallgrímur roared out at him, not even taking care to address him formally any more, 'Do you think you are capable of judging what's right and what's wrong in another part of this big country, a royal errand boy like you who's only been by the coast here for a day or two?'

He went on in this outrageous vein, but because more and more of it was in Icelandic, the Governor did not realize the full meaning of his words. The others managed to silence Hallgrímur and planned to use subtle means to pull him back into the seat that he had stood up

144

from in his excitement, but before anyone could stop him he had underlined his words by snapping his fingers rudely in the Governor's face across the table. That sort of gesture is understood by people of all nationalities, and is considered all the ruder, the higher rank of the nobleman who is subjected to it. Indeed, the Governor leapt to his feet, pale as a ghost now and shaking, saying that he would never have stood for such an act from a nobleman in Denmark without taking revenge, and far less would he tolerate it from an Icelandic peasant, whereupon he stormed away from the banqueting table and out through the door.

Those who were present and wanted to help Hallgrímur thought the best thing to do would be to spirit him away immediately, which was without a doubt the most sensible course, since word went around that the incident preyed so heavily on the Governor afterwards that he could neither sleep nor eat.

And when that noble man arrived for the Althing a few days later with his fine entourage, his cannoneers and his heralds and his drummers, he caught a glimpse of Hallgrímur in the crowd some distance away. He turned a different colour at once and was about to send his soldiers straight off to arrest him on the spot. But both Bishops and other men of high rank pleaded on Hallgrímur's behalf, but made little headway in making a reconciliation for him.

It so happened at that moment that some men who were with Árni Oddsson the Lawspeaker were heard to say that Gudmundur Andrésson was travelling not far away. And then it was Bishop Thorlákur who hit on the fine scheme that Hallgrímur should acquit himself of the Governor's wrath by the famous deed of chasing and arresting me. In the end he decided to try it, despite the fact that Bishop Brynjólfur, his brother-in-law, firmly advised him against such an ignoble deed and protested against the whole action.

Old Pétur had been told by his son, who was standing near to Their Lordships, that Bishop Thorlákur had not spared any colour in describing to the Governor what a danger this Gudmundur Andrésson posed to all God-fearing and moral people in Iceland, and the Bishop said it would take nothing short of a hero to arrest such a villain as me.

Also present was Sheriff Gudmundur Hákonarson, who spoke in the same vein and said that the entire foundation of law, all ancient precepts and ancient wisdom, would be in peril if action were not taken.

Pétur also told me, which I thought was noteworthy, that just as he was ordered to guard me he had seen Thorkell Gudmundsson, ready to leave, and he had ridden away from Thingvellir at that very moment. Perhaps I could allow myself the hope that this implied there would not be any more trouble. But on the other hand it could just as easily mean that they did not think there was the need for any more witnesses.

T here was truth in Pétur Gudmundsson the bellringer's words about the great wrath that the Bishop felt towards me: nothing was forgotten. When the Althing had been dissolved, but before the commencement of the grand banquet which had been proclaimed, two soldiers came up to the floor of the booth where I lay, pulled me to my feet and dragged me away, bound and fettered, then through the crowd in the direction of a large tent. I glimpsed several acquaintances of mine on the way, but none addressed me, with the sole exception of the Reverend Hallgrímur, who called to me in a loud voice that he would try to get Bishop Brynjólfur to intercede.

On reaching the tent, I saw Sheriff Gudmundur sitting outside on a beam against one of its walls, trying to make a small impression, which was not an easy task for him.

Inside the tent were the noblemen Bjelke and Akkeley, so that one mercurial figure was there representing the secular powers, and another the spiritual, the Vicar of God, Bishop Thorlákur. They were sitting at table, lapping wine from goblets, most certainly to induce hunger before the feast. To me they offered neither food nor drink.

For a while I stood there as they gazed upon me, then I collapsed from weakness and numbness of the legs, whereupon the soldiers undid my fetters and lifted me back to my feet. Their Lordships remained silent for some time, until at last the Captain addressed me and enquired, 'Have you written against the Great Edict?'

He was a portly man, his face smooth and unwrinkled, his nose roman and wonder in his eyes, rotund and broad-shouldered, quite possibly of the same age as myself, in his mid-thirties, although it is difficult to compare or equate such unlike species. He was well shaven, apart from the finely trimmed sliver of moustache which he wore on his upper lip, resembling more than anything else a pair of eyebrows, and a vertical strip of beard on his chin. The serpentine locks of his wig flowed over his shoulders and reminded me of a head of the Medusa which I had described in my *Rhymes of Perseus*, almost causing me to chuckle.

I chose at first to answer his question neither in the positive nor the negative, and acted as if I had been turned to stone, imagining the shrewdest course to begin by trying to hear how much they had been told behind my back. But then the Captain grew haughty and demanded of me, encircled as I was like Antiochus by Popilius' armies, that I either confess my guilt or deny it. I adopted the ploy of calling for the letter I had dispatched to them through the agency of the Reverend Thórdur Jónsson.

It turned out that the letter was there but had not been read by them, so it was now, for the first time, presented and read aloud, and translated into Danish. But those lofty men only shook their heads in laughter at those words and the Governor remarked that this could not satisfy them any more than a mere pinch of snuff.

I made a short reply in broken Danish that I felt I was within my full authority and entirely beyond reproach to exchange opinions candidly with my friends, but they retorted at once that this was unbecoming to the highest degree, called me sneaky and subversive and said that a worm such as I deserved to be held captive on the island of Seriphos. They laughed loud and long at this, and ordered that their goblets be refilled. Then Captain Bjelke turned serious again, shook his finger at me and said that from such an unspeakable offence I would not escape unpunished.

Until then I had said very little, having found it enough of an ordeal to understand what Their Lordships were saying, but now my temper flared and I spoke harshly.

'You do not know my writings for a fig, and you would not understand them either were they in front of your very eyes. What you have in your hands now is pure fabrication.'

After I had said this, Bishop Thorlákur made himself heard for the first time. He leapt to his feet and heaped all manner of abuse on me in Icelandic. This was the familiar rigmarole about my misdeeds of old and ever since, embellished in many respects which I detected at once to be the work of the Sheriff of Thingeyrar and his son.

I saw that I would have to control my temper if things were not to take a sudden turn for the worse. So I addressed the Bishop with the humblest of words, but he interrupted me at once with blatant mockery, calling my humility mere dissemblance and just as unbecoming of me as any other virtue. He picked up the tract which had been lying on the table, opened it and said, 'Here we have it all in writing and attested to, and since this is all so innocent and divine, it is only fitting for the author himself to defend what is said here.'

I saw the word *Theses* inscribed on the title page and even that outraged the Bishop, as he ranted at incredible speed against the contents of the tract, remarkably enough in Icelandic. As he did so he thrust at me pieces of paper on which he had scribbled down some of his arguments.

At first I was taken aback by such an intense display by this lethargic man who in general was respectable and not particularly excitable either, but I soon realized that he was paralytic drunk, and in fact had to steady himself against the table to prevent himself from staggering. Nothing would have been easier for me than to answer him and refute the absurd criticisms he launched at me, but I refrained, simply saying that I would answer nothing, since the tract was not mine.

'Even though it were,' I added, 'this is neither the time nor the place to debate it, for I am more dead than alive from hunger and the hardship I have suffered.'

And even now when I think back on this I must surely ask myself: Who, there and then, could have been supposed to pass judgment between myself and the Bishop? The Danes clearly did not understand a word of what was being said, but on the basis of probability and our gestures they must have concluded that the Bishop had demanded that I answered a particularly weighty matter and was incapable of reply.

I went on to invoke the spirit of the ancient court of Rome, saying, *Actori incumbit probatio* (it is incumbent on the instigator to prove the charge). At this the Danes pricked up their ears, having largely been preoccupied by their goblets up till then. The Bishop, on the other hand, answered me only with the preposterous words: Why should it be no less incumbent on the guilty to prove his innocence? When I told him this was not even worth answering, he snapped back, 'Somebody must have written this. Try to prove that you did not do it. We have been told that you are the man.'

'Yes,' I said, 'but there is no proof nor witnesses.'

The Bishop retorted, triumphantly waving the two pages that Thorkell had tricked me into giving him, 'Here is an insert that is clearly written with your hand, which I know very well, in fact far too well.'

And I again: 'But what if this is a draft, stolen from my study by treachery? It is none of my business what it says on another sheaf from somewhere else that is pasted after it. And both the people who circulated it are absent. The son has reputedly already had the good sense to leave, and his father is hiding somewhere outside this tent.'

At these words the Bishop's rage seemed to die down a little at last. For lack of witnesses he finally gave me a break, grudgingly though, threw the tract on to the table and banged down his fist on it, saying, 'Then come here at once and strike out all that you do not wish to acknowledge, then acknowledge the rest that you agree with.'

Sensing his hesitation, I made a bold bid to win a further postponement.

'I shall do that,' I said, 'when the time and place permit, but you must surely see, my Lord Bishop, that I have no chance of doing so after such rough treatment and in such a poor condition. And the second day of the Althing is over too.'

Before the Bishop managed to answer, the Governor was on his feet and had started speaking. Clearly he was beginning to tire of our wrangling. Of course he had not understood much of what the Bishop had been blaring out at me, apart from the occasional Latin term that the Bishop had used to embellish his speech, such as *schisma* and *h[ae]resis*, together with his accusations of breaking the law and insulting the authorities.

For all he could see and hear, it must have looked as if the great spiritual leader was faced with a trembling and speechless beggar and was flaying him alive. The Governor could not help imagining that everything that such a splendid man proclaimed and which enraged him so, backed up by the gigantic figure of authority who stood outside, was like a decree from the Temple of Jupiter and could not be anything but the purest of truths.

At which point he spoke to me, slowly and clearly and emphatically so that I could not fail to understand his ruthless words.

'I have more than half a mind to have you executed without trial.'

I knelt down and fell at his feet the moment I realized what he had said, imploring him not to take away from me something that he could never return.

Then he said, 'You may request to be allowed to stay alive for eight days, but you shall not go unpunished for longer than that.'

And I answered, 'You cannot be serious about intending to take a man's life without a trial. If I have offended against the King, I must surely be permitted to fall on my knees before His Majesty and beg his pardon. And if I am guilty of blasphemy I must likewise be allowed to refer my case to the Archbishop's court. I am ready and eager to do so of my own free will.'

He agreed that I should remain in their company, but, he added, as a prisoner. And that is precisely what I became there and then. He ordered the guards to clap me in irons and lead me away at once.

When I heard this I began to protest, determined not to yield, and emboldened by the fact that I had not been executed on the spot. I had also noticed that Bishop Brynjólfur was standing in the doorway now and had been listening closely to the last words we exchanged.

I insisted that the way they had concluded my case was not only illegal but also absolutely absurd. No reply came, and as the guards were about to seize me and lead me away, I turned to Bishop Brynjólfur as my last hope of salvation. I asked him his opinion, which he delivered at once, wise and reasonable as ever.

'It seems to me,' said Brynjólfur, 'that if Gudmundur is accused of having done something improper with his pen, then he should have the chance to take back his words in the same fashion, that is to say with his pen. There is plenty of paper here, do allow this man to write down what he feels.'

But that was out of the question. Their Lordships were thirsty and hungry and were eager to go to the grand banquet. Bishop Thorlákur called Bishop Brynjólfur a charlatan for trying to interfere in a matter that belonged under the See of Hólar. The guards dashed me away again and out of the tent. I was not allowed to say goodbye to my friends there at the Althing nor ask them to sign a statement clearing my name, to give me a shilling, a book, a testimony.

The guards lugged me straight away from Thingvellir and in the direction of Álftanes, beating me all the way and blaming me for making them miss the banquet. And when at last I arrived exhausted at Bessastadir in the evening of the following day, I was thrown into a dungeon.

Eight days after that the Governor returned, having finished his stay in the North with Bishop Thorlákur. He wanted to sail for Denmark at once, tired of this awful country with no roads in it, and reputedly eager to meet his mistresses in Copenhagen. Drained by hunger, I was at last rowed off in a shabby boat to the anchorage point and dragged aboard the royal guard ship, where the last thing I saw, before I was tossed deep down into my prison in the bilge water, was little Gísli, Bishop Thorlákur's son, and Headmaster Runólfur Jónsson promenading on deck ready for the voyage, both on their way to the University of Copenhagen.

Now I was sailing abroad too, admittedly, but not in the way I had long dreamed of, for a frightful voyage lay ahead of me now. All that kept me alive in my deep and watery grave on board there was the hope of just treatment in Denmark, where my case would surely soon come up before the Bishop and professors, and eventually before the King.

Since then I have been sitting here naked behind a naked wall, living on the bread of destitution for more than three months, and have not heard a single word from the authorities. On the poor writing paper which Fredrik the murderer mercifully procured for me, I have twice written letters to Bishop Brochmand, but have received no reply. Tears do such pain no justice, and I miss the different custom in Iceland, where our faith prohibits us from failing to answer letters. There, a single word will serve as a reply, and so will a character, cipher or deed, while only letters of outrageous content are returned unread. O Denmark, prove worthy of yourself, though I am unworthy of you!

What else can I do but adopt as my own the words of the long-suffering and sorely tried Job in the thirtieth chapter of his Book:

> *When I looked for good, then evil came unto me.*
>
> *And when I waited for light, there came darkness. My bowels boiled, and rested not: the days of affliction prevented me. I went mourning without the sun: I stood up, and I cried in the congregation. I am a brother to dragons, and a companion to owls. My skin is black upon me, and my bones are burned with heat.*
>
> *My harp also is turned to mourning, and my organ into the voice of them that weep.*

Now I can hear a key turning in a lock, my cell door opens and a parcel is tossed in to me, then the door is closed again and a bolt put across it.

Part Two

$\mathfrak{M}$ ost noble cleric, my best friend,
the Reverend Einar Arnfinnsson,
Stadur, Hrútafjördur

Without more ado or rhetoric I am writing to you now in the hope that you will receive this letter of mine on the first ship of the spring, and I feel as I jot this down that I must hurry, since I expect that you must be waiting with some impatience to hear of my lot, but particularly whether I am dead or alive.

Yes, my friend, I am alive, it is best not to delay telling you for another line, especially since the matter can be called your business too. Were it not for your intervention I would certainly have been dead long ago.

Yes, I have rarely rejoiced as much as in the third week of September last year when the guards in the Blue Tower promptly presented me with your letter dated August the fifteenth of the same year, together with some money and books, all received by those same guards in a single package delivered by the noble Doctor Worm's servant. Then for the first time the campaign could begin that eventually bore fruit in what I repeat: I am alive.

But it is best to tell one story at a time. After I had been taken away from the Althing without trial as the Governor's prisoner, I underwent a brief *process*: some rogues dragged me straight off to be imprisoned at Bessastadir, in what Jón Gudmundsson the Learned long ago called the Place of Torment, where I was left in wretched suffering for several days, until Captain Bjelke and his entourage

157

returned from Hólar and the ecstatic reception that had been arranged for him by his new-found friend, Bishop Thorlákur. Thereupon I was swept aboard the Governor's great frigate which lay offshore and crammed into a dungeon inside the hold. There I spent a wretched time in my own vomit and faeces while we sailed on a straight course here.

Whereupon I was promptly brought here to the King's palace, not straight to the King's feet in order to present my case to him without delay, but rather to the notorious Blue Tower where I was incarcerated. To cut a long story short, absolutely nothing happened in my affairs and I would doubtless have been left there to rot until kingdom come had I not received your welcome dispatch, your letter, and the knowledge that you had written to Doctor Worm himself and so cleverly drawn his attention to my affairs and the straits I was in, *item* by pointing out to him what benefit he could find from my scholarship, insight and poetic gifts.

How unspeakably relieved I was at this sign of life from you, which proved that I was not completely forgotten by everyone. Then I could begin writing again, and when I had procured some reasonable paper and a pen I took your advice and early in October wrote Doctor Worm a detailed account of the situation I was in, concealing nothing when I described the injustice I had been subjected to by the men of authority in Iceland, both the spiritual and secular classes.

Not long afterwards he sent me a reply saying he was ready to do everything in his power to further my case, which seemed to have come to a complete stop. The only thing that had been done was that Runólfur Jónsson and Páll Hallsson had been ordered to translate my *Discursus* into Latin for the Consistorium to examine, of course from the garbled and mad edition that derived from Thorkell's copy and which Bishop Thorlákur had pinned on Bjelke. It was useful that my original was among the things you sent me. Now I could send the correct text to the translators through the agency of Doctor Worm.

Next I wrote a letter to the Consistorium enclosing a document summarizing my defence, in which I described the course of events in much the same way as I had in my letter to Worm, although playing down as I could all accusations against Bishop Thorlákur, yes, even trying to glorify his part in most ways, hard as I found it, and presenting various points to his advantage. This was all done on Doctor Worm's wise advice, so that I would not instil those mighty theologians at the university with a sense that I had some particular aversion and opposition to the highest men of the Church and Christian faith in my country! By this time I could only hope that my case would begin moving, whether towards guilt or acquittal.

But this did not happen. The whole of October and November passed without my hearing a single sign of life, and the only news I eventually heard from Doctor Worm was that Runólfur and Páll had long ago completed their version of my *Discursus* which had been sent to the Consistorium. No more did that wise man know. So time went by and I am certain I would have died there from hardship and cold and hunger and mistreatment, had a ridiculous incident not taken place which unexpectedly solved all my problems.

I think I shall tell you the whole story in my own words, since you will doubtless hear something of it anyway, renowned as it has become among people here. It can only be said of this incident, just as I had mentioned in my letter to Doctor Worm, that much of what had happened in my affairs could be seen as amusing but tragic at the same time, like a comedy going beyond even what Menander himself could have imagined.

It was the beginning of December and I was sitting up on the windowsill of my cell, where I used to read when I was not prevented by the darkness and cold. But at this time my main intention was to watch the stars and motions of the constellations, for which purpose I used to slip my head and shoulders out between the bars. Since the weather was cold and I had little strength left because of my dull existence and meagre fare, I soon became tired and when I intended to pull myself back in I only succeeded in losing my grip and plunged from the window on the fifth floor of the Tower. All that I remember of my flight down was thinking that my final hour must have arrived. To tell the truth I did not regret it, given the pass that my affairs had reached, and thought the most fortunate outcome would be for me to fall all the way to the ground and be squashed there or drown in the canal, and thereby end my wretched life at the King's court.

But it turned out quite differently. Beneath my window was a gently sloping roof where I made a soft landing, not being particularly heavy after my deprivation in the cell. I soon managed to struggle to my feet on the rooftop and clamber up on to the rib, despite being rather dazed, and succeeded in inching myself towards the nearest wall where I could see a door which seemed to be my only means of escape.

I managed to crawl in through the door and the next thing I knew I was standing in a room where a scantily clad lady-in-waiting was lying face downwards on her bed with her skirts up, while a nobleman wearing a peruke was tupping her at his leisure from the rear. Their sport came to a sudden end when the visitor made his entrance, and the lady leapt up screaming from her bed and ran for the door as if out of her wits with terror when I modestly addressed them in as Danish-sounding words as I could manage, with my apologies for such a rude interruption, and said they should by all means continue going about their business because I desired nothing more than to return to my room in the Tower, and any idea of villainous deeds or escape were the last thing on my mind. But the man with the peruke, imagining that Sir Satan himself had come, turned pale and pleaded for mercy as he slid under his departed mistress's bed, where he inadvertently kicked over a grand porcelain chamberpot brimful with the most aristocratic of urine. That splendid artefact broke on impact and committed that priapus to a watery grave under the bed.

Commotion broke out in the building. I heard women howling from all directions and the crying of royal children. Everyone thought I was a ghost or a monster, and indeed I did not look an appealing sight, covered in filth and still wearing the same cowl I had on when I was manhandled in Kaldidalur. It emerged that I had landed, in this tragicomic manner, in the living quarters of the royal family itself, and that it was the nanny of the royal children whom I had so brashly intruded on and disturbed in her bed. The whole building was thrown into turmoil and a rumour went around that the prisoners in the

160

Tower had made a mass break-out. Nor did I have to wait for long before a troop of guards appeared, armed to the teeth and ready to finish off the evil escapers. But they could hardly hold back their laughter when they saw what they had to deal with: that at their feet lay only a single Icelandic beggar, more dead than alive from deprivation and terror, and pleading for nothing more than to go back to prison. And they were no less amused when the nobleman crawled out from beneath the bed, trembling and naked from the waist down, with his peruke soaked in urine and his eyes rolled back to the whites as he begged their assistance in like manner.

Once the situation had been clarified, my wish was granted and I was taken back to my cell without any recriminations. But the outcome of this absurd and embarrassing episode was that my case was expedited more than all the intervention of fine men had been able to manage until then. For while all this was going on the King happened to be sitting down to dinner with several of his friends from the cream of the nobility, including my accuser, Captain Bjelke. When the commotion spread through the rooms, Their Lordships immediately asked what had happened. And when the truth came to light and was told as an amusing story at table, Governor Bjelke stated that the man in question must have been his Icelandic prisoner from the previous summer, Gunder Andersen, and that it was a miracle he should still be alive. This prompted the King to enquire about my case, which proceeded quickly after the Consistorium began investigating it.

That high council made its ruling on the twelfth day of December *anno domini* 1649 and this was submitted to the King along with my *Discursus*, *item* my document of defence. In their ruling the learned theologians said they had read my tract, but it transpired that they had nothing else to say of it than to regurgitate what they said Bishop Thorlákur had written in a letter to Bishop Brochmand of Zealand. No, not even those learned men were allowed to reach their own conclusion! The chorus leader himself had to start up the song. In the said slanderous letter from the Bishop of Hólar, I am described as a ruthless criminal whose writings aim at leading simple fisherfolk astray by defending unrestrained wantonness, fornication and incest in breach of the Great Edict which has been endorsed by the most God-fearing King Fredrik the Second. The Bishop claims I have been incited to this by the Devil and in particular used the technique of misusing the Holy Scriptures with cunning references and interpretations. He requested of the authorities to ensure that the said villain Gudmundur should have no chance to return to his fatherland, where no good could ever come of him.

The learned members of the Consistorium said they agreed with Bishop Thorlákur's cited words in each and every respect, since every detail that the Bishop reproached and condemned was stated and proved many times over in my writings, together with many scathing remarks that rightly appal Christian minds and ears.

Of my document of defence, they said they did not feel confident about passing judgment. Of which I only say that they certainly never read it.

When the King had pondered this ruling for twelve days (but with other business besides, I expect) his conclusion was the same: I should be released with no further recrimination if I signed an undertaking that they had composed for me. In it, I agreed that I had not only pursued a highly unbecoming and wanton life in my fatherland, but had also compounded my unseemly behaviour by discussing it in speech and finally in writing.

Then I undertook on pain of punishment never again to incite the wrath of God with such discourse, as I had so evilly done until now, nor to propagate it improperly with my pen. Neither to allow myself ever to be found in my fatherland for as long as I live (whether I may walk again after my death they did not specify), and if it is ever proved against me that I have behaved or acted against His Majesty's aforementioned mercifully stated terms of clemency or against my own signed undertaking, then I shall be clapped in irons at Bremerholm as prescribed, without any expectation of being granted royal pardon.

Yes, dear friend, this was the Christmas treat that Their Lordships served up for me, and once I had signed that sentence of exile the hospitality that I had enjoyed in the Blue Tower came to an end and I went out on to the streets of the city without a penny to my name.

162

Never having felt worse solitude than that day, I went to church to listen to the Christmas service and was fortunate enough to run straight into several compatriots who are studying here. They took me in and gave me food and a place to stay for Christmas night. Their main figure was Runólfur Jónsson, who has treated me splendidly ever since.

Just after Christmas I went straight to see Doctor Worm, knowing that he was favourably disposed to me and had done what he could to draw attention to my case, though all his efforts bore less fruit than my fall out of the Tower window. The good Doctor welcomed me, and I have been able to get by on what I have earned for various tasks he has given me.

I have survived reasonably and have enough to buy food and drink and tobacco, although my work is sometimes intermittent. Yet I am somewhat plagued by the uncertain outcome of all my affairs here, and plagued most of all by the knowledge that I cannot go back to Iceland alive. Though that may turn out well later. I foresee some hope ahead.

No more of that, I hope to be able to write some joyful news to you in the course of the summer.

So I shall finish this letter, dear friend, and try to get it aboard ship. I trust you will send my greetings to everyone whom you know that I know. I don't care about the others. I hope to hear from you when the first ships return here from Iceland. I also eagerly await news of my nearest and dearest.

To your health,

Copenhagen,
the fifteenth day of April, *anno domini* 1650
Your lifelong friend,

Guðmundur Andrésson

y best friend, noble cleric
the Reverend Einar Arnfinnsson,
Stadur, Hrútafjördur, district of Húnavatn

Receive herewith the outlaw's annual sign of life. Thank you for your
fine letter of last autumn and also thanks for all your kindness towards
my impoverished mother. I desperately await news of her situation,
such as whether she is still in charge of Bjarg, and if so, who is working
for her.

Of my own situation, this is the main news. The hope that I felt I
foresaw last year, as I hinted, has richly come to fruition for me and it
is true to say that the wheel of my fortune has spun full circle. I was
admitted to the university on June the twelfth last year, taken into
college as a resident and started studying eagerly. My *praeceptor
privatus* is Vitus Bering, a great poet and scholar, an arrangement
made on the advice of Doctor Worm, who thought it more propitious
than taking me on himself. He mentioned that our dealings together
were so close that it would be healthy for me to have other supporters,
not putting all my eggs into one basket.

In other words I have done much work and am still working on
ancient Nordic scholarship for Doctor Worm. I have made some Latin
notes to the rune chapter of the *Sayings of the High One*, from Stefán
Ólafsson's useless translation, and further more many criticisms of his
even worse translation of *The Sibyl's Prophecy*, where my patience
eventually ran out and I opted to translate and annotate myself, all in
Latin, for which I was praised by Doctor Worm. I have also copied out

and summarized a great amount from Icelandic writings, such as those on Greenland, with which the doctor is particularly fascinated. I also made a copy of *nomina propria Gothica, Runica, Islandica et Septentrionalia* for Jørgen Seefeld, the judge in Ringsted, and was rewarded with no less than twenty-four thalers.

Runólfur Jónsson has continued to help me greatly and become a particularly good friend of mine. He has now had printed his great essay on the languages of the North, *Lingvae Septentriolis elementa*, and appended to it my poem *Runa reclamat*, which is a great honour. The same will happen later this year when Runólfur's *Grammaticae Islandicae Rudimenta* comes off the press: I again am given the honour of having a poem printed to accompany his work, this time as a preface. I call it my *Lullaby for the Ancient Relics of the Northern Tongue*.

The Regent's College is a good place to stay, although the fare is rather meagre. It does not affect me personally too much, since I demand little in the way of food, besides which I have my excellent income from all my scholarship which Their Lordships like and are prepared to commission from me. So I have always been well stocked with tobacco and drink since I came here; the beer is one of the best things in this city. Sometimes too good.

They often joke, my masters here, that I am like a writing machine when the mood takes me, saying the most suitable thing to do would be to lock me away somewhere with ink and a pen and toss inside tobacco, beer and food to me, like a pig in its sty. With such an arrangement, they say, I could easily sit writing until kingdom come.

As you can see I am well satisfied and you might think that I do not care a fig for the exile to which I was sentenced. That is not so. However, it causes me unspeakable discontent to be forbidden from returning. Not because I want to go home – I certainly would not go though I were able to; it is simply the thought of not being able to if I wanted which weighs me down.

I hope this letter of mine greets you in good health and spirits and with it I also impose on you the duty of sending my greetings to everyone you suspect would accept it. Occasionally I chance to think of Frída and my son. You would not happen to have heard any reliable news of their fate? Do you see my mother? And what news is there of our friend Björn from Skardsá?

May you live in full health at all times.

Copenhagen,
the first day of May, *anno domini* 1651
Forever your friend,

Guðmundur Andrésson

y best friend, honourable cleric
the Reverend Einar Arnfinnsson,
Stadur, Hrútafjördur

I sincerely hope it did not trouble you too much not to receive a letter from me with the spring ship last year. Certainly, however, you must have heard of my situation from some of the people who came out here, and thereby knew that I was still more or less alive. I hope you have not feared too much for my life. I did come very close to passing over as I lay sick in body and mind, but through God's mercy I recovered well in the summer after the weather began to improve. In particularly I bene-fited from the medical skills of our friend Thorkell Arngrímsson, who has been here and in the Low Countries studying much in those arts.

On recovering my health I have continued to study eagerly. On Doctor Worm's express advice I have largely given up spirits and tobacco after being subjected to his personal and strict reproaches and persuasions, which he jokingly calls his 'detoxification'. I find myself much freer and clearer of mind after having banished those two demons. So I have been able to allocate some of the money that I formerly spent on such things towards dressing myself better, in continuation of which I have become more respectable, since I am now *decanus* at the tenth dinner table.

I have held two disputations at the University, *De principiis rerum natura* and *De elementis*, both chaired by my friend Runólfur Jónsson who is now a *magister* and held in the highest regard. I enclose them herewith for your entertainment.

167

And who would have believed it: one of my best companions here is little Gísli Thorláksson, the one who stole the silver spoons so long ago. He holds me in great honour, is very willing to learn about ancient lore from me and eagerly accepts my help on theological questions and interpretations. His father ought to hear that! Gísli, as it happens, is a fine fellow, although not exactly a man of character and unlikely to become Bishop. But who knows, nepotism takes itself seriously.

Outside the college, I am working mainly on compiling a large lexicon of the Icelandic language, which many people in Denmark have long been eager to see produced. Doctor Worm has been striving for me to undertake the work. Until now nothing of this sort has been available apart from the dictionary of the ancient language by the Reverend Magnús from Laufás, while the intention behind my book is to record words from all periods, ancient ones as well as the language spoken in Iceland today. This will be a big book with Latin glosses of all the Icelandic words, tracing their origins all the way back to Hebrew where possible.

It is my hope that I shall live to complete this book; it is no easy task to put together such a compendium, matching each item with the other and arranging everything felicitously.

I shall not make this letter much longer, but hope to be able to send you the printed and published book within not too many years.

These days I think little about being, in effect, an exile. Nor after I heard the news of my dear mother's death last year is there much that ties me to that rock, far away in the ocean, called Iceland. And I have abandoned all hope that my son is anywhere to be found. So there are not many people up there whom I could call my nearest and dearest. Only friends such as you.

Páll Hallsson came back here last year after spending a year at Hólar, where he lost all the toes on both feet from frostbite and had to support himself with two walking sticks. He is much better now after Doctor Worm whittled his feet into a better shape. But I could not help reflecting that I could have thought myself lucky to lose only my toes in that land of ice. I'll be damned if Blefken with all his wild accounts about Iceland was the dolt that people claim! I expect I shall settle here contentedly now that things have come to this pass, and I hope to end my days here as a royal lion of scholarship. Doctor Worm says there is a good chance that I will, if I strive to study and work and let all wantonness pass me by.

Vale semper,

Copenhagen,
the third day of May, *anno domini* 1653
Your lifelong friend,

Guðmundur Andrésson

Noble cleric,
> the Reverend Einar Arnfinnsson,
> Stadur, Hrútafjördur

Now that the ship is to sail for Iceland I cannot delay telling you of the death of your old friend Gudmundur Andrésson, in the pestilence which this year has continually harried here in Copenhagen and beyond, and to which no end appears in sight.

It was towards the end of March that Gudmundur fell sick with the illness, like so many of our countrymen when it struck at the Regent's College. He stayed alive for only a few days, then fell asleep for the salvation of his soul on the first day of April this year. I heard this when I returned here recently after spending the winter in Leyden in the Low Countries. Before then, his praiseworthy patron Professor Doctor Ole Worm had fallen sick with the pestilence and died, not having spared himself in tending to the sick and suffering who are to be seen everywhere. The pestilence also claimed the life of *Magister* Runólfur Jónsson, who was Rector of the college in Christianssund.

Knowing of the old friendship between yourself and the late Gudmundur, and also that he felt himself to have no stronger ties to anyone in Iceland than you, I felt myself obliged to inform you in full of this matter.

I also want you to know that Gudmundur had acquired the finest reputation here before he met his end, and was considered to have found his right path in life in all respects, which doubles the tragedy of his loss. He was increasingly working for Doctor Worm around the time of his death on a large dictionary of the Icelandic language, in which he explains not only much ancient diction but also many words which are on the tongues of common labourers in our country even today. What will come of that great work I do not know.

May you live in health and send my greetings to any of my relatives back home whom you chance to meet.

Copenhagen,
the fifth day of May, *anno domini* 1654

Thorkell Arngrímsson

Part Three

𝕴 cannot be called a remarkable man. Yet I often have the impression that people think I have now taken a remarkable if not very fortunate course in my life, by leaving my farm and family to seek news of my long-deceased father whom I never saw when he was alive. But why? Only the ignorant ask that.

My name is Skeggi Gudmundsson, generally known as Frída's son Skeggi in my youth. It is almost the middle of the month of perpetual daylight, in the morning of the fourteenth day of June, *anno domini* 1684, and I am thinking these things at Stadur in Hrútafjördur, where for the moment I have been enjoying the hospitality of the elderly and noble cleric and scholar, the Reverend Einar Arnfinnsson, and talking to him in his study.

Who am I? Less than half a year ago or so I would have had no trouble in answering that question. I would have said I am the farmer from the West Fjords that I am, poor, admittedly, but earning a steady living, married to an honest and God-fearing woman, and the father of two promising children. I would have said that then and in fact would not be lying were I to say it now. Yet in truth I feel I no longer know who I am, and so it has been for almost half a year, ever since the great affliction of mind came upon me last.

It was the beginning of last February when, unexpectedly one dark morning, this repulsive affliction poured over me and ran through my whole body, chilling my bones to the marrow and sapping my strength and stamina. Admittedly I have had this tendency during the darkest part of winter for many years now, but have always blamed it on the magic tricks of my neighbour Bersi the Sorcerer and the visitations and evil demons he has sent against me. All the previous attacks, however, were only ever brief ones, though intense, and always ended when my aged mother, who has been living with us, sent for old Bersi and gave him a gift in return for releasing me from the spell at once.

But this year I did not expect any harm to come to me, since Bersi the Sorcerer was burned at the stake towards the end of the previous winter, praise be to God and our energetic witch-hunting Sheriff, Thorleifur Kortsson, and I was not aware that anyone else had taken over the old man's magic arts and absolute hatred for me. But all this came to nothing. At the appointed time the repulsive affliction seized me as usual, except that the attack seemed much fiercer than ever before. And what was worst and barely comprehensible, there was no Bersi around any more to release me from my burden.

This is what happens. The repulsive affliction instils me with the idea that life is not lived for any purpose. All my worldly toil until now seems like mere vanity – happiness and sorrow alike. Everything becomes one. Ahead of me lies darkness with no prospect of brightening. Even my nearest and dearest, my wife, children and mother, I no longer feel the slightest concern for them. Thus I gradually sink down into lethargy and brooding which in the end becomes paralysis, and my mind goes a blank. By that time I have long before stopped getting out of bed for any other purpose than to relieve myself, preferably in the middle of the night to avoid meeting anyone. Otherwise I lie silent and motionless, staring at the walls. Sometimes I will accept a cup of whey or spoon of curds that someone may bring me, generally my wife Rósa.

When I had been lying bedridden like this for more than two months without changing my clothes, and with no cure in sight, I heard my mother and wife talking about what to do about my illness. I could not hear properly what they were saying, although I could hear the sound of their voices, but I knew what they must be talking about anyway, because they never discussed anything else when this happened. Suddenly they fell silent, and then my mother said, 'He has it from his father, that's the trouble.'

At these words the haze seemed to lift from me. This single

sentence cut its way through the fog and struck something living which woke my mind so that my heaviness moved away. I realized that, for the first time, I had heard my mother mention my father. My interest was aroused, and so I knew that my illness would wane, because while it lasts I do not find anything worth thinking about. Then it dawned on me that my illness and madness could not have been caused by old Bersi, nor ever had been on the previous occasions. My mother had obviously not believed this either, but only cunningly used the old man's reputation for sorcery to drive away the gloomy disposition which she knew ran in the family, as had now come to light. I felt betrayed. I felt a slight pang of conscience about Bersi being burned at the stake. As it happened there were plenty of other reasons for doing that, since there were charges against him from many places, but I have always been puzzled by the way that sorcerers' skills seem to fail them in escaping the flames. Did they maybe never have any skills, and if so, why burn them then? Or is this a manifestation of the true nature of Devil, who betrays his most servile underlings at the moment of reckoning? The backbiter who would not bite back. But it should not be forgotten that old Bersi readily and willingly confessed to it all, and the strength of his repentance was mentioned in particular.

After this I got back on my feet but still felt a peculiar emptiness within me, as if my own personality had vanished. But at the same time my conviction started to grow that the answer to the question of who I was would never be found until another question was answered: Who was this Gudmundur, my father?

His name was Gudmundur Andrésson, I knew that much, well known in his day for some writings – I never found out what they were, but soon learned that they were considered quite scandalous and incurred the disapproval of God and good men. My mother never wanted to talk about him and she made me realize, when I was growing up, that I would do well to keep my paternity to myself. Yet he was a learned man.

Suddenly I could not help picking up occasional remarks about him, and from those fragments I formed my own impression of that man, vague as it was. I filled in that impression with a few details which I managed to squeeze out of our old Vicar, Thorlákur, so that the outcome was something like this.

Gudmundur was born around 1615 at Bjarg in Midfjördur, the ancient home of Grettir Ásmundarson the Strong, the son of poor parents. Somehow he managed to be admitted to school. He attended Hólar, where he matriculated, but he could not go abroad to study on account of his poverty, was never ordained as a Vicar and lost his prospective bride, because he had offended the Bishop with his sharp and exceptionally insolent writings, besides being suspected of sorcery. He had been a Deacon somewhere for a few years, however, but was not even allowed to keep that position because of the Bishop's ill will towards him. Afterwards he seems to have worked at Bjarg to provide for his mother, who lived there in her widowhood, but he also did some teaching at households where people did not object to his reputation. Early on in this period he wrote a pamphlet containing embarrassing jibes about the Bishop and his family, and thereby dashed his own chances of reconciliation, ordination and office.

But whatever hope he had, it was certainly reduced to nothing when I appeared. I am born in sin and my parents were sentenced to pay a fine under the Great Edict. After that my father had no hope of ever becoming a Vicar. He wrote a violent attack on the Great Edict, the morality law itself, and made so bold as to oppose a law that had been passed by the Althing and confirmed by the King. He received his just deserts, the Reverend Thorlákur said. He was sentenced to death.

That was the only knowledge I had when I decided to abandon everything in the middle of the haymaking season and journey to Stadur to visit the Reverend Einar, who was said to have known Gudmundur better than any other man.

have been staying at Stadur for the past few days, hearing from my learned and noble host, the Reverend Einar Arnfinnsson, all the main things he could tell me about my late father, Gudmundur Andrésson, from his own acquaintance and what Gudmundur had told him. Archdeacon Einar also showed me some books and letters which he has in his possession and concern Gudmundur. I have either read them myself or had Einar translate for me the ones that are written in foreign languages.

Thus I have read his writings against the Great Edict, which he called his *Discursus oppositivus* and for which he paid the ultimate price. Shocking as it may sound, I must admit that in my heart I agree completely with every word it says there and am proud to have had a father who dared to stand up against the injustice that is some times dealt out from above.

Now I am returning home, much the wiser, and I feel I am closer to my original question: Who am I?

I have often felt, while listening to Einar speaking, that Gudmundur himself was standing right there beside us, talking to us, and I have dreamed him during those nights there and felt I could enter into his thoughts. As I stand here ready to leave, a quite remarkable portent has appeared which the Reverend Einar claims is a belated greeting from my father to me. A consignment has just arrived from Copenhagen, on board the ship that had docked at Höfdi, and was brought over to Stadur. A parcel containing a book addressed to the Reverend Einar, which turned out to be Gudmundur Andrésson's great dictionary, his *Lexicon Gudmundo Andrae*, published in

Copenhagen last year, *anno domini* 1683, by the revered Doctor Resenius, who Einar says is a man of great renown. The Reverend Einar gave me this book as a parting gift, saying that he did not have much longer to live himself and the best thing would be for me to own it.

With that greeting from my father, I am returning to the West Fjords, to my home.

MARE'S NEST

Mare's Nest brings the best in international contemporary fiction to an English-language readership, together with associated non-fiction works. As yet, it has concentrated on the flourishing literature of Iceland. The list includes the three novels that have won the Icelandic Nordic Prize.

The poetic tradition in Iceland reaches back over a thousand years. The relatively unchanging language allows the great Sagas to be read and enjoyed by all Icelandic speakers. Contemporary writing in Iceland, while vivid and highly idiosyncratic, is coloured and liberated by this Saga background. Closely observed social nuance can exist comfortably within the most exuberant and inventive magic realism.

181

Brushstrokes of Blue
The Young Poets of Iceland

Edited with an introduction by
Pál Valsson

112 pp. £6.95 pbk

'Exciting stuff: eight leading northern lights constellated here'
Simon Armitage

Sigfús Bjartmarsson   Gyrdir Elíasson   Einar Már Gudmundsson
Elísabet Jökulsdóttir   Bragi Ólafsson
Kristin Ómarsdóttir   Sjón   Linda Vilhjálmsdóttir

A representative introduction to contemporary poetry in Iceland,
Brushstrokes of Blue is full of surprises, from startling surrealist
juxtapositions and irresistible story-spinning to gentle *aperçus* and
the everyday world turned wild side out.

Epilogue of the Raindrops

Einar Már Gudmundsson

Translated by Bernard Scudder

160 pp. £7.95 pbk

'A fascinating and distinctive new voice from an unexpected quarter'
Ian McEwan

Magic realism in Iceland is as old as the Sagas. Described by its
translator as 'about the creatures in Iceland who don't show up
in population surveys', *Epilogue of the Raindrops* recounts the
construction (and deconstruction) of a suburb, the spiritual quest of
a mouth-organ-playing minister, the havoc wreaked by long-drowned
sailors, and an ale-oiled tale told beneath a whale skeleton, while the
rain falls and falls and falls.

Justice Undone

Thor Vilhjálmsson

Translated by Bernard Scudder

232 pp.   £8.95   pbk

'Thor Vilhjálmsson's hallucinatory imagination creates an eerily beautiful vision of things, Icelandic in far-seeing clarity, precision, strangeness. Unique and unforgettable.'
Ted Hughes

Based on a true story of incest and infanticide and set in the remote hinterland of nineteenth-century Iceland, *Justice Undone* is a compelling novel of obsession and aversion. An idealistic young magistrate undertakes a geographical and emotional journey into bleak, unknown territory, where dream mingles sensuously with the world of the Sagas.

Angels of the Universe

Einar Már Gudmundsson

Translated by Bernard Scudder

176 pp.   £7.95   pbk

'Einar Már Gudmundsson, perhaps the most distinguished writer of his generation, is generally credited with liberating serious writing in his country from an overawed involvement in its own past, and with turning for inspiration to the icon-makers of the contemporary world.'
Paul Binding, *The Times Literary Supplement*

With humane and imaginative insight, Gudmundsson charts Paul's mental disintegration. The novel's tragic undertow is illuminated by the writer's characteristic humour and the quirkiness of his exuberant array of characters whose inner worlds are gloriously at odds with conventional reality.

Night Watch

Frída Á. Sigurdardóttir

Translated by Katjana Edwardsen

176 pp.   £7.95   pbk

'She has written a book that has no equal in recent Icelandic literature.
It is remarkably well written and tells several stories
that all merge into one . . .'
Susanna Svavasdóttir, *Morgunbladid*

Who is Nina? The capable, self-possessed, independent,
advertising executive, the thoroughly modern Reykjavík woman?
Or is she the sum total of the lives of the women of her family,
whose stories of yearning, loss, challenge and chance absorb her
as she watches by the bed of her dying mother?

Trolls' Cathedral

Ólafur Gunnarsson

Translated by David McDuff and Jill Burrows

304 pp.   £8.95   pbk

'It is a vagrant, morally unsettled form of story-telling on the same
wavelength . . . as Dostoevsky.'
Jasper Rees, *The Times*

'*Trolls' Cathedral* is a formidable work, mesmerically readable.'
Paul Binding, *The Times Literary Supplement*

The architect yearns to create a cathedral echoing the arc of a
seabird's wing, the hollows of a cliff-face cave. His struggles with debt
and self-doubt appear to be over when a seemingly random act, an
assault on his young son, destroys him and his family. Obsessions,
dreams and memories lead, inevitably, to violence.

Nominated for the 1998 International IMPAC Dublin Literary Award

The Swan

Gudbergur Bergsson

Translated by Bernard Scudder

160 pp.   £8.95   pbk

'For many days after reading *The Swan* I remained preoccupied and enchanted with it. Here is a great European writer who has, with extraordinary subtlety and in a unique way, captured the existential straits of an adolescent girl.'
Milan Kundera

A nine-year-old girl is sent to a country farm to serve her probation for shoplifting. This is no idyll: she confronts new and painful feelings and faces the unknown within herself and in her alien surroundings. By submitting to the restraints of rural life, she finds freedom.

Z – a love story

Vigdís Grímsdóttir

Translated by Anne Jeeves

280 pp.   £9.95   pbk

' "I want you to know the real me" resounds tragically through this novel . . . To be afraid to finish reading a book is a strange feeling, but *Z* grips the reader with peculiar force.'
Marín Hrafnsdóttir, *Dagur-Timinn*

Two sisters, Anna and Arnthrúdur, seek to understand themselves, each other, their lives and their relationships with their lovers – with Valgeir, semi-detached from his wife, and with Z, the journalist named for the flash of lightning that attended her birth. Approaching death casts issues of independence and commitment into sharp focus as the women's contemplation achieves a blistering and loving honesty.

William Morris

Icelandic Journals

216 pp.   £15.99   new edition, cased

The *Icelandic Journals* are pivotal in Morris's aesthetic, political
and literary development. He was fascinated by Iceland and his
experiences there helped to clarify his ideas of the relationships
between function and beauty in design and between art and labour.
His translations of the Sagas and the vocabulary he evolved for them
influenced his late fairy tales.
The Journals were last published in England in 1969.

The volume has a foreword by William Morris's biographer,
Fiona MacCarthy, and an introductory essay by Magnus Magnusson.
The illustrations include facsimile pages from the original edition and
endpaper maps of Morris's routes.

'For Morris enthusiasts these journals are invaluable. For one thing,
Morris kept a diary only occasionally, and this document of his
thoughts on a day-to-day basis, during a critical time of his life,
proposes one of the most accurate portraits available to us . . . the
journals are an engrossing and sympathetic insight into one of the
planet's most fantastical countries . . .'
Simon Armitage, *The Spectator*

'The Sagas alone people Morris's Iceland. His beautifully simple but
detailed accounts of the landscape are heightened by his knowledge of
what happened there . . .'
Glynn Maxwell, *The Times*